# VIKTOR

## The Petrov Family

**DARCY EMBERS**

Copyright © 2023 by Darcy Embers

All rights reserved.

No portion of this book may be reproduced in any form without written permission from the publisher or author, except as permitted by U.S. copyright law.

This book is a work of fiction. Names, characters, businesses, organisations, places, events, and incidents are the product of the author's imagination or used fictitiously. Any resemblance to actual persons, living or dead, is entirely coincidental.

Cover design: Canva

Formatting: Atticus

Editor: Enchanted author co.

Proof-reader: Enchanted author co.

| | |
|---|---|
| Authors note | V |
| Dedication | VII |
| 1. Viktor | 1 |
| 2. Amaia | 11 |
| 3. Viktor | 21 |
| 4. Amaia | 25 |
| 5. Viktor | 29 |
| 6. Amaia | 34 |
| 7. Viktor | 39 |
| 8. Amaia | 45 |
| 9. Viktor | 55 |
| 10. Amaia | 61 |
| 11. Viktor | 65 |
| 12. Amaia | 73 |

| | | |
|---|---|---|
| 13. | Viktor | 83 |
| 14. | Amaia | 87 |
| 15. | Viktor | 93 |
| 16. | Amaia | 97 |
| 17. | Viktor | 103 |
| 18. | Amaia | 111 |
| 19. | Viktor | 119 |
| 20. | Amaia | 125 |
| 21. | Viktor | 133 |
| 22. | Amaia | 143 |
| 23. | Viktor | 157 |
| 24. | Amaia | 167 |
| 25. | Viktor | 173 |
| 26. | Amaia | 179 |
| Epilogue | | 187 |
| Acknowledgements | | 195 |
| Also By Darcy | | 196 |
| Petrov family | | 197 |

# AUTHORS NOTE

THIS WAS ORIGINALLY A novella for a Christmas anthology and would have been book 3, although they can be read in any order as a standalone.

Viktor contains explicit and graphic content for readers ages 18+

Please be aware that this novella contains talk of body dysmorphia, everyone with this condition struggles differently. This is my own minimalized experience and feelings while battling it myself. If I ever release this as a more in depth novel, it will have more experiences. As this is a novella, I wanted to keep it brief.

This book may have scenes triggering to some, for full details please visit the authors Instagram.

www.instagram.com/authordarcyembers

# DEDICATION

To those who enjoy getting tied up and pleasured by a man who wants to own you.

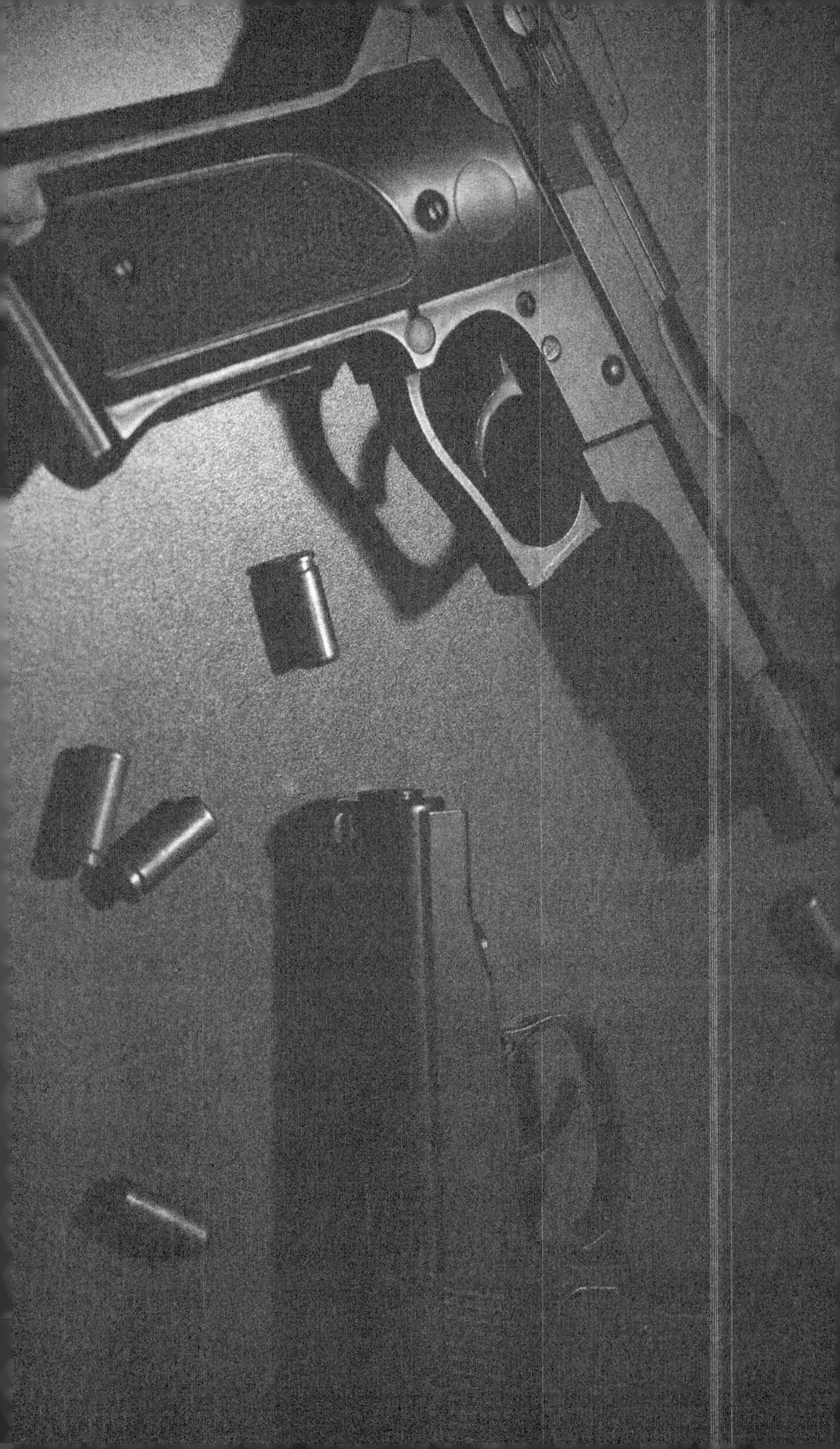

# Chapter One

## Viktor

Staring down at the two women on the white sheets of the bed as they breathe heavily in bliss, I tuck my cock away in my pants. The brunette moans, "Don't put it away, I don't want to be done. Those piercings felt incredible."

I chuckle; my Jacob's ladder always makes the girls scream. In a good way, of course.

"I have business to attend to," I tell them.

Someone had been stealing from me, and I wanted to sort this myself. This is personal to me, and my men know it.

A treaty of arranged marriage ended the war after my mother was murdered. The only thing I hear about them is how the Koskovich woman is a bitch. At least I didn't have to marry her, but it had obliged me to hire a new man. I had tried to keep him away from most of the business, leaving him to serve as only a drug courier, with no access to most things, or so I thought.

Now, it's time to fix it.

The blonde tries sitting up, but her wrists are still tied to the bedpost. She pouts, her lips slowly curving into a smile. "Come back when you're done? I'll wait right here." She pushes her tits out temptingly. As enticing as it is to nibble on her nipple, I've got to go.

With a smirk, I unbind her and carefully put my tie back on. I run my hand over the fabric to smooth it out as much as possible, shrugging when it doesn't yield.

"See you another time," I mumble as I turn away, leaving their little bag of ecstasy on the table.

The door shuts heavily behind me, and I step out into the quiet corridor. I don't trade sex for the drugs; they still pay. I fuck them because they were sexy as hell and up for a threesome. It had been a while since I'd had an offer like that.

My phone rings as I reach the elevator and press the button, and I let out an annoyed sigh. If only I could do this another night and stay in bed, it would be perfect. Instead of internally complaining too much, I press the screen to answer while I step inside.

Konstantin, my right-hand man, has been giving me updates on the whereabouts of Dmitri Koskovich, the cousin of Svetlana. The family we went to war with over killing my mother.

"We found him. He'll be at a ballet show tonight," he tells me as a greeting.

You'd think it would be easy to locate a traitor, but Dmitri has been lying low ever since I found out he had been replacing my drugs with painkillers. I refuse to let it get any further.

Konstantin asks, "Do you think he will tell us anything? Or that we'll even get the thousands of dollars he took?"

"Doubt it, but I have a bad feeling, and it's time to clear out my employees. My clients don't deserve the shit he's been dolling out." It's frustrating; my time is being wasted. Now Dmitri is the most recent man I'm going to have to kill.

"Why did you even bother giving him any extra work?" Konstantin questions. My jaw clenches.

"You know I didn't want to. It's a friends close and enemies closer type of deal. Since his family killed my mother, every time I see his face, I want to tear him to pieces. But I haven't yet because of keeping the peace between families." It's a shame I won't be able to drag it all out like I want. I need him to confess and tell us everything.

"Fair enough, boss, the others will be at the venue to collect while everything is set up in the warehouse."

"It won't take long." With that, I hang up. Konstantin is used to my bluntness, after all. I'm sure he won't mind.

The elevator doors ping at the ground floor, and my leather shoes tap on the ground as I stride through the lobby, nodding to the employees as I leave. They do it back, and I smirk; I love getting the respect I deserve.

People had always seen me as irresponsible, 'the party boy' of my family, which is how I got into the drugs side of the business. I had always loved the idea of working in sunny California. When my father gave me the chance to run in this area, I took it. The conditions being that I put my partying days far behind me.

I still have my fun, just not as much. I'm no longer sampling the product or sleeping with every woman possible. I do drink, but I don't get drunk. I had always hoped to make my father proud. Now is the time I feel I really am doing something.

A warm September breeze brushes over me as I step outside into the busy Beverly Hills street, the valet brings my black Lamborghini around for me as I'm waiting and when he steps out, I slide in after he hands me the keys. Once I'm comfortable, I search inside the glovebox for the ticket to the ballet show Dmitri will be at.

Truthfully, I didn't see him as the type who had an interest in dance, but I shrug to myself anyway, memorizing the address for the theater.

Putting my car in gear, I crawl away from the hotel. Speeding down the long roads, weaving in and out of traffic, until I finally pull into the valet space at the theater and chuck my keys at the guy. He grins as he looks at my car.

"Scratch it and I kill you," I warn, and his face pales when he takes a better look at me, realizing who I am. He nods and slides in slow and carefully.

My eyes scan all the people outside the old, but still beautiful building with pillars either side of the door where tickets are being collected. Finally I see the tall man with dark-brown hair and a short trimmed beard. It's Dmitri; I notice him walking into the theater with a dark-haired woman hanging off his arm, fawning over him in his black suit and tie. He has too much confidence for a man in his position.

Internally rolling my eyes, I follow. I need to wait until he's on his own, so I go to the well stocked bar and order a couple of drinks before we all go in and take our seats on the ground level for the show. Finally, he stands to leave the venue, pulling a box of cigarettes from his pockets without looking behind him. When he reaches the door, I down the rest of my drink and follow him. Once we are out of the crowds in the night air, I grab him and drag him out of sight, shoving him up against the dirty wall.

Dmitri struggles to fight me until the light illuminates around us. When he sees my face, he goes white. "You're here for me?" His voice trembles.

Stepping closer, I shove him against the wall a second time, knocking the air from his lungs.

My words are full of venom as I speak to him. "You stole from me. You know what this means. The treaty for us? It's over." I grin.

"Fuck," he mumbles, his head tipping back on the wall. Did he really think he wouldn't get caught? "It wasn't much, just skimming off the top," he tries to reason with me, hands held up as though he can stop me, but I'm unforgiving.

I go with a theory that has been running around in my head.

"Don't play dumb with me. You are losing me clients and building your own base. Ivan must be back now to rebuild what you lost, but I promise you. After everything, your family will never gain power. They are coming back, wanting to take over. It's not happening."

"What are you going to do to me?" His shaking voice sends a small echo into the darkness of the night. Luckily, the traffic of people bustling about the city drowns out the noises coming from this pathetic man.

My savage smile grows. "You get to try my new product, make sure it's ready for the market." I pluck the little bag out of my inner pocket, revealing the skull-shaped pills inside, and hand it to him.

"Right now?" he asks, a bead of sweat building on his temple under the dim alley lights when he steps further into the wall. His hands shake as he opens the small plastic pouch and places the unusual pill on his tongue and swallows it dry.

I harshly grab his face and check that he has taken it.

Then I lean in to tell him the truth with a chuckle, "No one fucks with the Petrov family. You killed one of my men to get what you wanted. You're going to tell me everything I want to know."

I had laced the pill with a large percentage of sedatives, so he'll be unconscious for me in no time. I smile like the Cheshire cat when he realizes what's happening.

His eyes widen as he panics, trying to push me away and shove his fingers down his throat to get it out. I hold him up against the wall with my forearm as he struggles. Quicker than I expected, he sags against me.

I wait for the black van to pull up at the entrance to the alley, a couple of my most trusted men jump out and drag Dmitri inside. I'll get my answers and dump his body. The police in my back pocket will blame another dealer if he is found.

But it makes my life easier if I chop him up and send off his parts to the rest of the family. They will get the right message.

I brush the non-existent dirt off my suit jacket with a sigh as the men close the doors to the blacked-out car.

Taking a deep breath, I walk back inside, curious about these dancers he had come to see, so I don't go in the direction of the bar. I act as though I belong there as I walk through to the backstage area.

That's when I hear muttering from a side door near the stage. A place I shouldn't be wandering, but I approach the door anyway. I can't help myself and push it open slightly. I take a peek in the gap to find a beautiful woman with dark hair pulled up in a bun wearing a full ballerina outfit, stretching against a horizontal bar.

I step closer, pressing my hand against the door frame as I lean in. The frame creaks slightly at my weight, but I don't care, my eyes raking over her body. *Maybe I will stay for a while.*

She turns and gasps upon noticing me. I raise a suggestive eyebrow. Her eyes widen, and she storms over and slams the door in my face.

Feisty. Just the way I like them. I lick my lips. I'm going to have her.

All I need is a little bit of time to make her want me too. I turn back and soon return to my seat in the audience, making myself comfortable.

The lights dim, curtains open, music starts, and there she is.

I lean back and enjoy the show. Her tight little body bending in ways I didn't think was possible. It's making my pants uncomfortable as my cock strains against the zipper. Fuck, I need to know who she is.

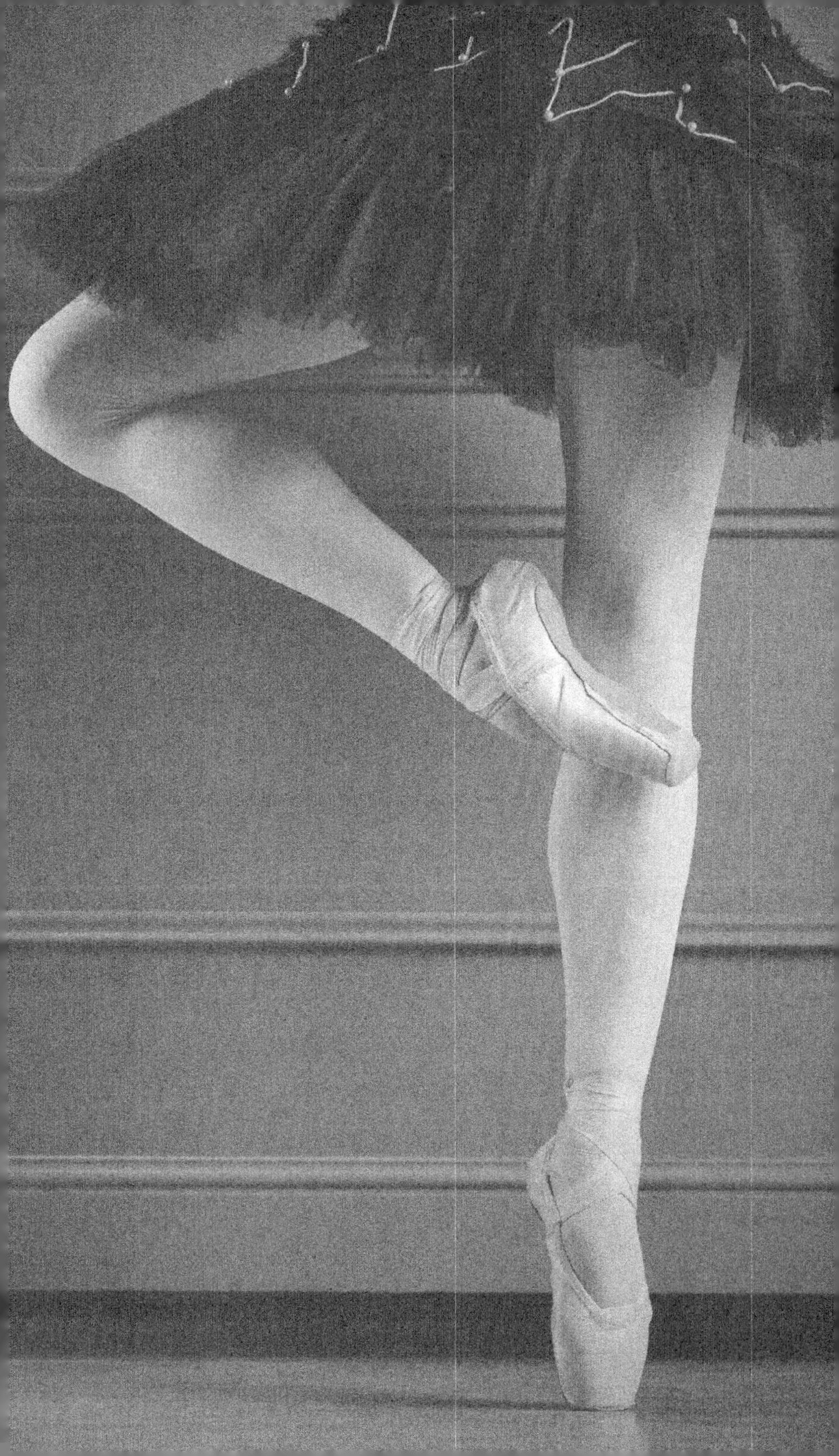

# Chapter Two

## Amaia

I try to forget the man at my dressing room door earlier as I glide along the stage. I look out to the audience from the side stage and can't find my half-brother Dmitri anywhere. He promised he would be here. I wouldn't have bothered sending him a ticket if I knew he wouldn't show up.

I tell myself he had business to attend to and couldn't text me, because I'm not dumb enough to brush off that he works with bad men sometimes. For one of the most violent families I had heard of, but thankfully never seen.

Things were bad around ten years ago. I was young then, so I never fully understood. My mom kept me away, and I never saw my dad after that, the only thing I had heard was that he had been involved in a family feud. I'm guessing he died. Dmitri found me a few years ago, I guessed he was involved with bad people when he had bodyguards follow me. I complained. He hated it. Now I spend most of my time training. Ballet is my life. Nothing ever happened to me, he got less paranoid and eventually he called them off and learned my daily routine instead. Which hasn't changed in years.

The man who was watching me at the door made me feel uncomfortable; he looked every bit like a predator about to pounce. The shadows across his jawline with a smirk almost hidden made my heart beat a little faster. It's been a while since I had been attracted to a man, as I tend to avoid them during show months, but he appeared out of nowhere.

Manners told me to excuse myself and close the door gently, but I couldn't. It was an intense and charged moment. He would become a distraction, and I needed him out of sight.

I need to get back in my headspace. The next dance is coming up, and I can't fail. I've been training for hours daily to become the Prima Ballerina. I'm in my prime, and if I don't get the position soon, I won't ever become one. This has been my only dream in life since I decided that being on a stage, under lights, while moving my body in a way to tell a story, is what I'm born for.

Luckily, the other dancers don't notice my trembling as I stand in the left stage wing, waiting to go out for our next song. "You'll do great," Damien whispers.

*Focus.* Lights, music, and showtime. Deep breaths, remember my dream, and let my body flow.

As I dance, a calm settles over me, and I stay in the moment I've trained for. Many eyes are on me, but I'm used to it.

Though I can't help but feel a new gaze landing on me, and only me. One that is setting fire to my veins, and I don't hate it. I push the thoughts away as the crescendo approaches, the movements flowing through me easily.

Each pirouette spinning to perfection. The small jumps across the stage until I reach my usual partner, Damien, who lifts me. I breathe through it and pray that skipping my meals for the day will make me a little easier to lift. His arm wobbles under my weight, and that's when I realize a day wasn't enough. I need to lose just a few more lbs.

After hours of dancing have passed and we've gotten changed to leave, Damien approaches me while running his hand through his sweaty blond hair, and I hold my breath. I don't need him to mention the struggle of our lift.

"Are you okay?" he asks. "You seemed a little stiff tonight." A breath of relief leaves my chest; he didn't mention it.

Forcing a smile, I lie, "I'm fine." Not wanting to be reminded that Claudia, our trainer, will punish me for it. Nothing but perfection in her shows. And tonight, I was sloppy. Distracted.

He presses his hand against my lower back as we walk out the doors. "Come out for a drink with me?" he suggests, raising an eyebrow with a cute smile that most ladies would fall for.

"You know I don't drink during show week," I chastise.

"Just one, to relax?" he pushes, flashing another charming smile, the one he always gives me when he asks to spend time together.

I sigh, knowing I probably need one to sort through my feelings and what I'm going to do to stop my emotions eating me from the inside out. My mom made me join ballet when I was seven, so I could learn to control my emotions. She didn't want me to get any violent tendencies from my dad, but it's still there. Deep down. I just became better at hiding it.

"Where did you have in mind?" I ask, finally giving in, even though it didn't take much convincing. At least it isn't food.

He grins. "Just at the bar in the hotel. We won't need to rely on taxis and can stay as long as we like in case you change your mind." He shrugs.

I bite my lip. I know he has a crush on me, as he keeps hinting towards a date. But I don't date much, especially with another dancer. It's too messy. I should say no and stop leading him on, but after everything, I really need to relax and have that drink.

"Just one. Then I need to rest or I'll be awful, and Claudia will never let me forget it. I've already screwed up tonight." I deflate as we head toward the hotel. It's late, and the streets are quiet. I enjoy the silence.

Damien holds out his arm for me to take, but I ignore it and stroll towards the doors with my bag clutched to my body. He follows close behind, luckily not mentioning any hostility I'm holding onto right now; he will likely brush it off like usual. I don't mean to be awful, I just need him to get the hint that I'm not interested. He needs to move on.

Inside, we sit at the bar and order our drinks, and I try to rush mine without being rude. I insisted that we didn't need a private table like Damien had wanted.

My gaze searches the rest of the room while my fingers tap along to the faint music in the background, praying for other dancers to join us. Damien is a nice guy. He just isn't for me, even if we weren't dance partners. He would be too boring, I want fireworks. Damien is just... not that. He deserves a nice girl. Someone worthy of his kindness.

There are eyes burning into my body as I sit on the stool at the bar taking another sip of my cocktail. I just know someone is watching me, and what's worse is that I *know* who.

My eyes flick around the room again. That man from earlier stands opposite me at the bar. My palms start to sweat as he walks closer, his eyes never leaving mine. I rub my hands down my dress subtly.

My head swings back to Damien; it's time for me to leave. I feign a yawn. "I've got to go to sleep. Thanks for the drink. I'll see you tomorrow?" I rush to say and hurry away before Damien can get a word out.

I can practically feel his disappointment, but I can't stay. I'm praying he doesn't follow.

I stab the elevator button multiple times as though it might make it come faster, muttering under my breath, "Hurry up." The numbers go down too slow to get to this floor, and I resist the urge to tap my foot from impatience.

My heart races as a shadow looms over me from behind, heat emanating from whoever the large body belongs to as the figure steps closer.

My eyes scrunch shut, and I need to even out my breathing before he notices. I refuse to turn around to see who it is. But my gut is telling me it's the same man following me. I hold my breath as the bronze doors ping open, a group of giggling girls pushing past as they leave in their drunken state.

I step in, and I can see him in the mirror behind me. Our eyes connect, and his darken as he follows me inside. I suck in a breath; he's devastatingly handsome up close and out of the shadows with his strong jawline and jade-green eyes burning straight through me.

He looks like he could be one of those dangerous men my brother works with. It's not safe, and I should run. Take the stairs, go to reception.

But it's too late. The doors have closed.

"Floor?" his deep, husky voice asks, and warmth spreads throughout my traitorous body as it's clearly responding to him. It's been too long since I've last had sex. That must be it, absolutely nothing to do with him.

"What?" I blurt, turning towards him, attempting to ignore all the warnings firing through my brain right now.

My face is heating underneath my makeup, and I hope he can't see.

He gestures to the numbers of each floor on the buttons, and I let out a breath of relief and press the button for my floor. Then I pull my phone out of my bag to text Dmitri, hoping the stranger doesn't talk to me anymore; a great distraction to kill my libido is my brother.

Before I know it, the doors ping open, and I look up.

"Goodnight," the mystery man says as he saunters out.

I check the floor number. We are not on the same one. Thank fuck for that. My head drops back against the mirror wall behind me, and I chuckle to myself as the doors close. I'm being paranoid.

When the door to my room shuts behind me, I take off my dress and throw it on the floor, stripping off my bra and panties next, which join my outfit. Then I grab my products from my suitcase and take a shower.

The large mirror opposite taunts me. Every time I see myself, my eyes zero in on all my imperfections. A bit of extra fat between my thighs, my lower abdomen has too much of a pouch. I turn away in disgust. It's okay, I'll skip lunch tomorrow.

I stand under the hot water, letting it cascade over my body. Massaging my aches from the show. Washing away all my thoughts of the day and then disappear down the drain.

Eventually, I force myself to leave the steaming shower after a few moments of simply standing there and wrap myself in a white towel. Then I rummage in my suitcase until I find something to sleep in, and I shove on the tank top and shorts, dropping into the bed with my damp hair spreading out around me.

Exhaustion wraps around me and pulls me under just as the first sounds of rain patter against the window.

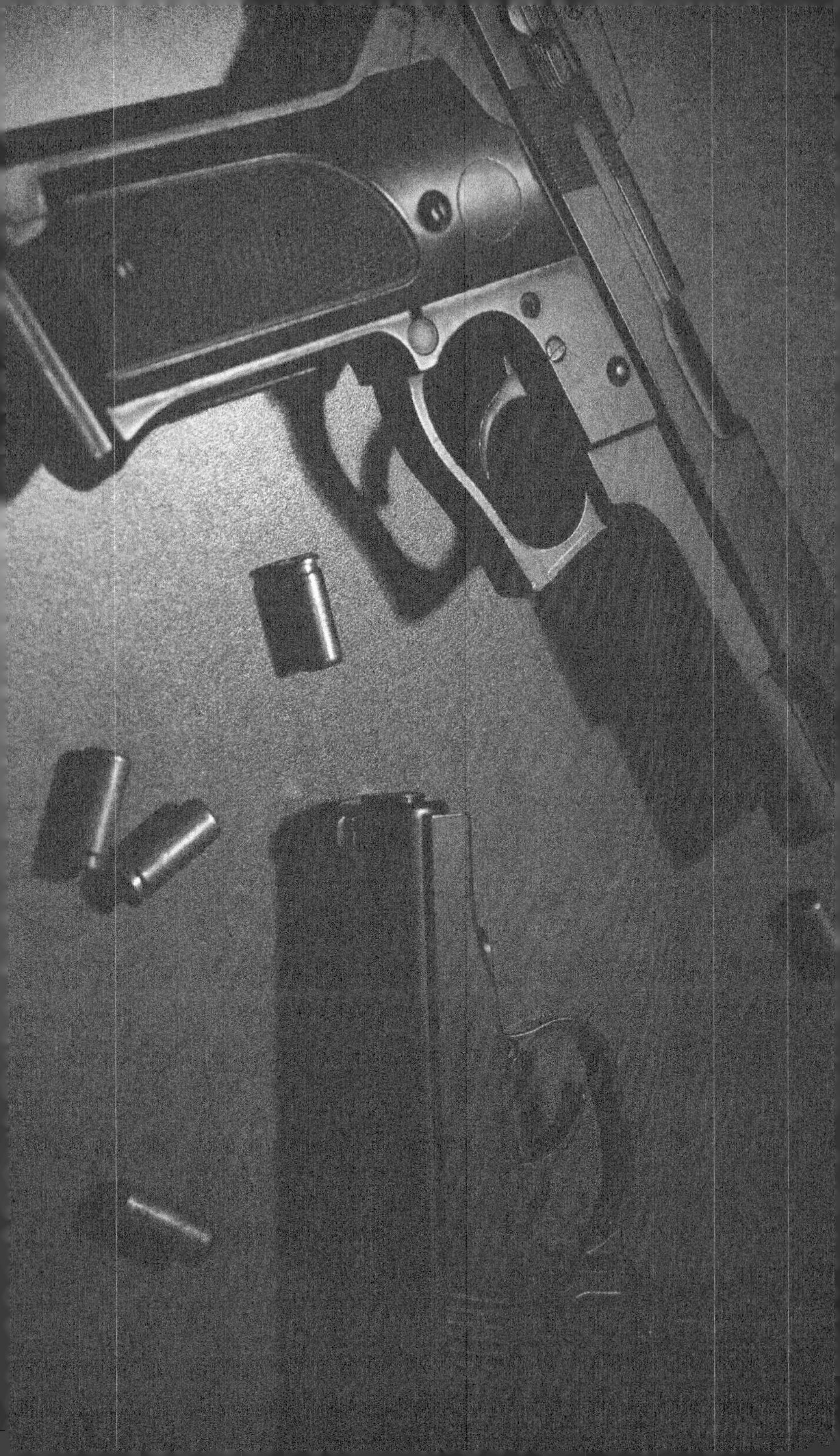

# Chapter Three

## Viktor

Her chest rises and falls as she's in a deep sleep. She was captivating up close and out of that cute little outfit from on stage.

I had to get closer. Watch her. Get to know her habits and win her over.

She won't be as easy as the others, and that's what will make her taste better. She's too good for a man like me, but I'm going to ruin her for anyone else. I'll be imprinted on her mind and body.

She had been relaxed with that other man; he clearly wants her. She doesn't seem to return that sentiment, if the strained smiles she sent his way were any indication. But I still had to know if he came back here with her at any point.

It wasn't hard to find someone's name in the system when I fucked the receptionist, Kassie, not long ago. All

I had to do was tell her I needed to check some things and since my name is big around here, she didn't question it. Those love hearts in her eyes as she stared at me almost made me run. I don't like the idea of settling down just yet. Not for another couple of years.

I found that a group of ballet dancers are staying here for the weekend, and a copy of their driver's licenses are in the system. Booked in for just one more night for the shows.

Amaia Frost.

That's her name. I roll each letter over my tongue to get used to it. Unique and just as beautiful as her.

I leave the lobby quickly and swipe the housekeeper's keycard from the office to sneak into Amaia's room, not being able to help myself. I enter silently with a glass of scotch. I only like shots of Vodka with a meal.

It's silent in here as I stalk toward her. Dark brown hair fans out on the pillow, her pink lips parted and emitting soft snores while her tiny frame only takes up a fraction of the bed. As I get closer, I twirl a strand of damp hair between my fingers and the coconut shampoo reaches my nose, overpowering the alcohol on my breath.

She rolls onto her side, and I drop the strand, stepping toward the curtain to open it a fraction. Allowing in a sliver of moonlight for a better view of her, the glow making her pale skin seem ethereal.

My eyes scan the room, and I notice her scrunched-up panties, I lift them to my nose and inhale her scent. Intoxicating. Satisfied, I take a seat in the corner of the room just to watch her as I finish my drink and place the empty glass on the table. Then I unzip my pants and pull out my cock, wrapping the pink silk around my length and pumping in my hand, each barbell of my piercing making me more sensitive. I have to hold in my groan as I watch her chest rise and fall, nipples pebbling underneath her tank top as she wears no bra.

How I'd like to suck on one and hear the moans come from her pretty mouth. It's not long until I'm throbbing and my cum spurts all over her panties and my hand. I drop them next to my empty glass for her to find when she wakes. When I tuck myself back in, she starts to stir. It's time to leave.

The door clicks softly as it closes behind me.

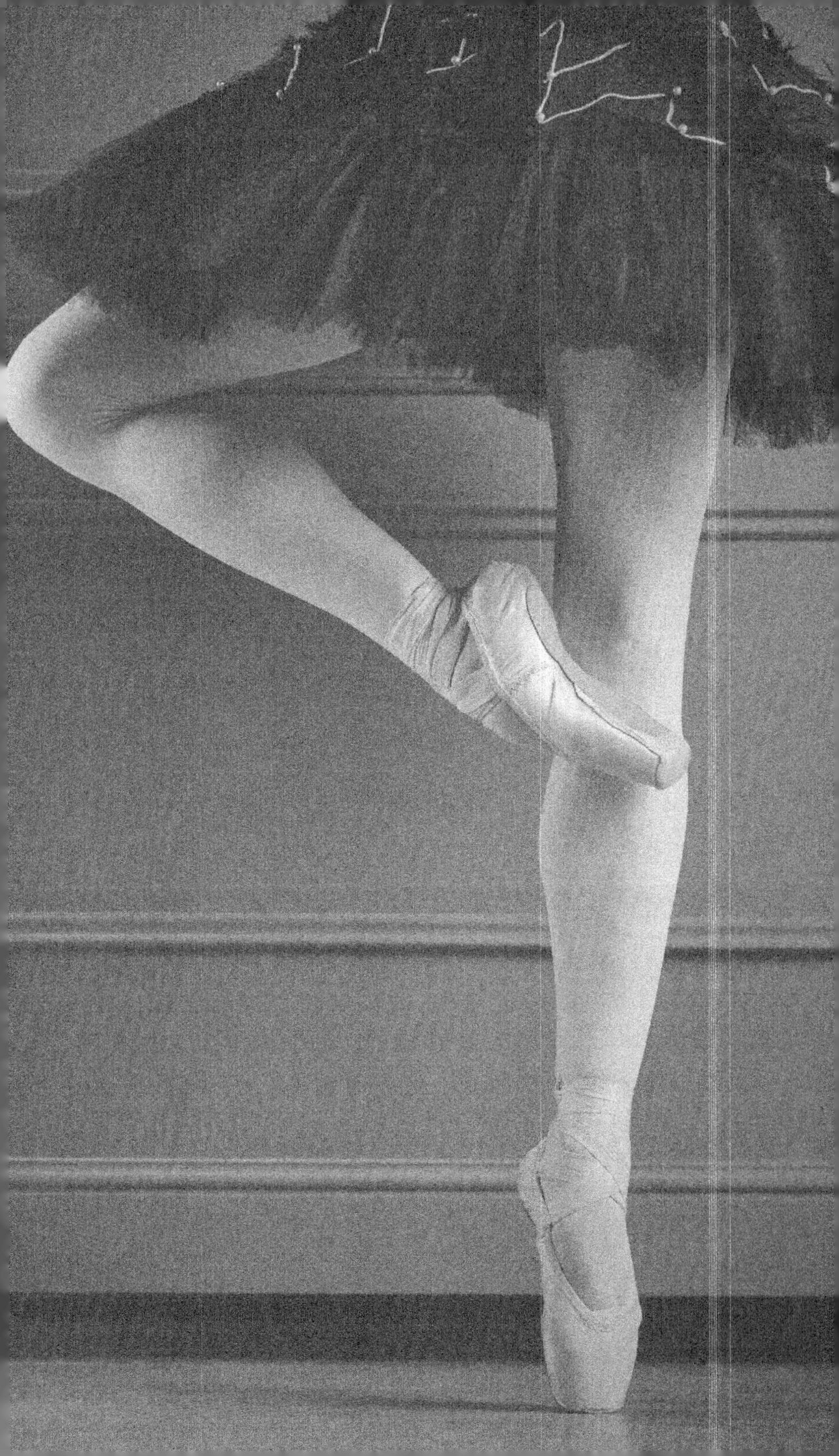

# Chapter Four

## Amaia

The sound of a moan pulls me from my sleep, the full moon shining through a gap in the curtains. I move to get out of bed, but the door to my room makes a noise. I slam my hand against the light switch on the wall next to me, rushing to get it on, but not taking my eyes away from the darkness in front of me.

The room is empty. I sigh and lean against the headboard, letting out a deep breath.

Until I see an empty glass on the desk next to a ball of pink fabric. *I hope that's not what I think it is.* Sliding out of my bed, I hesitate to move toward it. My heart is beating fast. I call out, "Who's in here?"

There's no response. I sneak across the room on my toes to stay as quiet as possible.

"I have a gun. You should leave now." I don't actually have one, but hopefully whoever it is doesn't want to be shot.

I lift the glass and sniff it. Scotch. It's not my drink of choice—ever. Someone else was here, I don't know who it could be. Picking up the pink and *wet* fabric, I drop it again. I know exactly what that is.

I don't sleep for the rest of the night, too afraid the intruder will come back.

---

My face looks awful. I cover it up as much as possible with makeup, but I can still see the dark bags under my eyes. I tie my hair up and rush to the studio. It's our last rehearsal before I get to go home and have a break from being on stage for another few weeks. Usually, I look forward to the breaks, but knowing that I could lose my chance as Prima, I need to be here. Show them how committed I am.

"You're late!" Claudia calls as I rush to the changing rooms, and I stiffen. But then I paste on a fake smile and make eye contact with her.

"My alarm didn't go off this morning. I'm sorry." The lie slips easily from my tongue.

I'm always awake early, but considering I never actually slept, there is no excuse for me to be late. Except needing to sneak out of my room and peek around corners, skipping the elevator just so I don't bump into this man.

She shakes her head. "You're better than this. Go and stretch."

Damien gives me a sympathetic look and mimes *what's wrong?*

But I merely shake my head and look back at Claudia, who squints at me, waiting for an answer. "Yes, ma'am," I say.

Thankfully, Claudia doesn't correct me too much. I try to relax my body, but last night still haunts me. What would he have done if I'd woken up while he was still there? Did he touch me?

I shake my head to snap out of it. Surely, I would have known if he had.

Concentrate, deep breaths. Regain control.

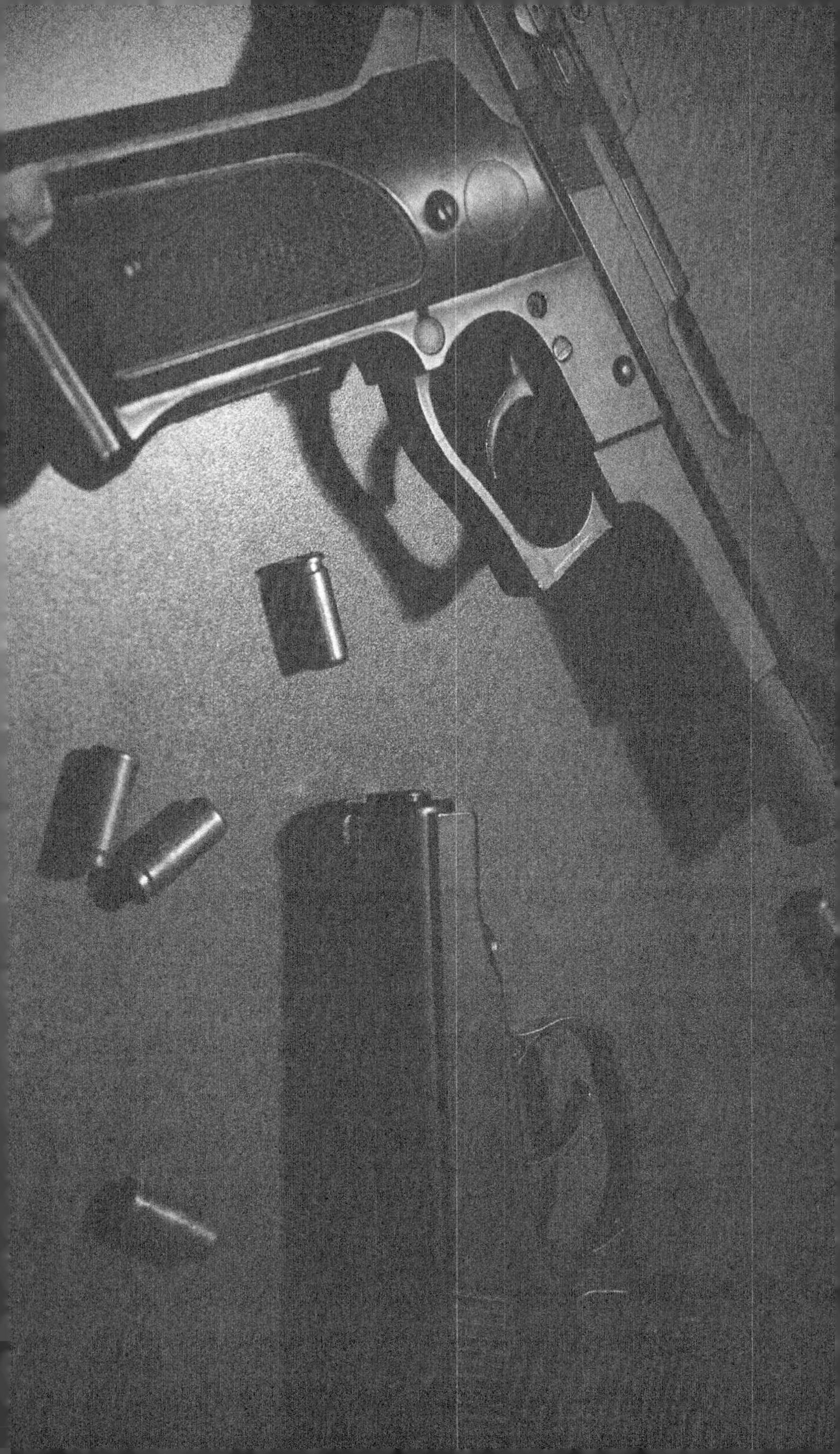

# Chapter Five

## Viktor

I watch her from afar this time as she dances across the stage, overshadowing everyone else up there. The way she is lost in the moment. I've never seen a woman like this. In control.

I want to take that away from her. Bring her back to my house and in my spare room with a modified bed reserved for *special* guests.

I've already noticed she had checked out of the hotel this morning. She doesn't live too far away, so I'm surprised she even bothered to get a hotel. I'm assuming it's to keep all the dancers together, since I noticed that they had all booked rooms. Fuck knows I don't know anything about ballet.

Konstantin did a basic background check on her and she lives alone. Perfect. It's all I really wanted to know. I already went there earlier today to check the layout. It's just an average-sized house with one bedroom. The studio she goes to is not far from hers. The only security she has is a chain lock from the inside. Good for me, but I will have to rectify that in the future so no one else can get in there. One thing I did notice was that some files of her background check had been hidden. She's a mystery I want to unravel and I can't wait to find out.

I bring my thoughts back to the show, ignoring the vibration of my phone in my pocket. Konstantin can keep an eye on Dmitri a little longer. Give us the extra time to break him down.

Amaia's face is smooth and flawless under the lights as she moves. I wonder how long she's trained for to become this perfect.

Even though she isn't center stage. To me, she is the star of the show. The sight of another man's hands on her body as he lifts her makes my jaw clench, his hands too close between her thighs. I'm not usually a jealous man but want her; she will be my little doll. And I can't wait to play with her.

After the show, all the dancers bow, and the audience applauds them. That bastard has his hands all over her again, and she looks uncomfortable as he wraps his arm around her waist and pulls her to his side, but she doesn't say anything. He continues to pull her closer just as the curtains close.

My fists clench until my knuckles turn white. Abruptly, I stand, pushing my way through the crowd. Most of them move, already knowing who I am. Now it's her turn to find out.

Getting backstage is easy. My little doll turns to me with a smile, but it instantly drops and her eyes narrow. All I can think of is how she looked sprawled out on the bed, sleeping. I smirk, and she turns away. She'll get used to me soon. Right now, I'll just watch as she moves toward the changing rooms.

The innocent-looking ones are always the dirtiest and I can't wait to find out how filthy she can be.

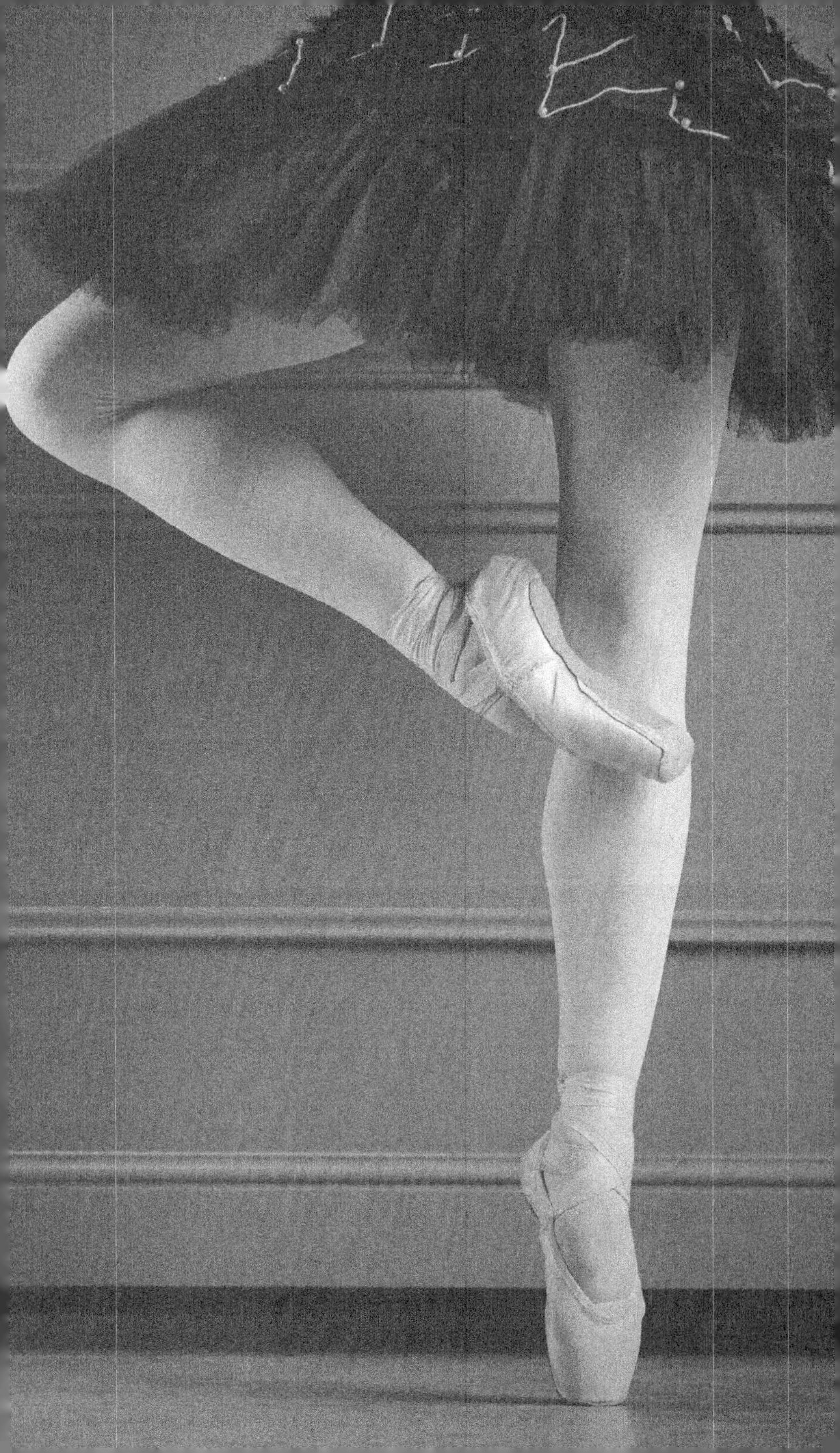

# Chapter Six

# Amaia

I slip on my basic black dress over my stockings with the small penknife tucked in them. Since that man snuck into my hotel room, I've always kept one on me. I'm not sure it was specifically; it's just a hunch. He is the only new man in my life that has shown any interest and I can imagine him having no boundaries. I've heard of him; the words Mafia and drugs are hushed around. One of the Petrov men. He is powerful and violent. He is a man never to be crossed.

And somehow, I have gained his attention.

He watches me from the bar as I leave the changing rooms, people passing me pink roses and telling me how my épaulement was perfect. I'm polite and give them my practiced smile. Until he stands in front of me, handing me one red rose.

A breath gets caught in my throat as I look up into

those deep green eyes. He smiles, displaying white teeth. My smile never wavers even though I'm nervous around him.

"You were spectacular out there," he tells me with a slight accent, and now I'm calmer; I realize what it is. *Russian.*

"Thank you, sir," I start, but he leans in to kiss me on the cheek, his heady cedar scent rushing over me.

He murmurs into my ear, "Viktor. Remember it. You'll be screaming it soon." His warm breath against my sensitive neck causes goosebumps to spread over my body before he pulls back.

I can't stop the heat pulsing between my legs. I'm surprised my jaw hasn't dropped at how open he spoke to me like that, then has the audacity to wink at me.

Damien comes over and wraps his arm around my shoulders, plucking the rose from my fingers. My eyes roam back over Viktor, and his smile has gone. I clutch onto Damien's arm, he stares down at me, waiting.

So, I wave toward Viktor to introduce him. "Damien, this is Viktor. He is just telling me how much he enjoyed the show."

He puts his hand out to shake with Viktor, but he stares between each of us for a moment before reaching out his own. Damien makes a strangled sound as Viktor grips his palm. "I'll pick you up later," he mumbles, giving me a peck on the cheek before he walks away, leaving me alone with Viktor again.

"Is he your boyfriend?" Viktor asks, taking a sip of his amber drink. Scotch.

"He might be." I shrug.

He leans in close, his mouth brushing the shell of my ear. "I don't think he is."

My face scrunches up and I pull away. "What?"

But Viktor doesn't answer.

"I don't even know you," I can't help but spit out. Who is this guy, and what does he want from me? I should stay away; he is dangerous, after all. My mouth opens to speak, but words about my brother are on the tip of my tongue. Dmitri hasn't answered my calls, and he won't be able to go up against Viktor if I make him angry.

That's when it hits me. If I don't mention Dmitri and handle this myself, it will keep my brother safe. We have different last names, so no one will connect us, and our dad is gone.

But I still have his blood running through my veins. Surely, I can protect myself. I'll just need to find a new angle.

A smile stretches across my face. Sex.

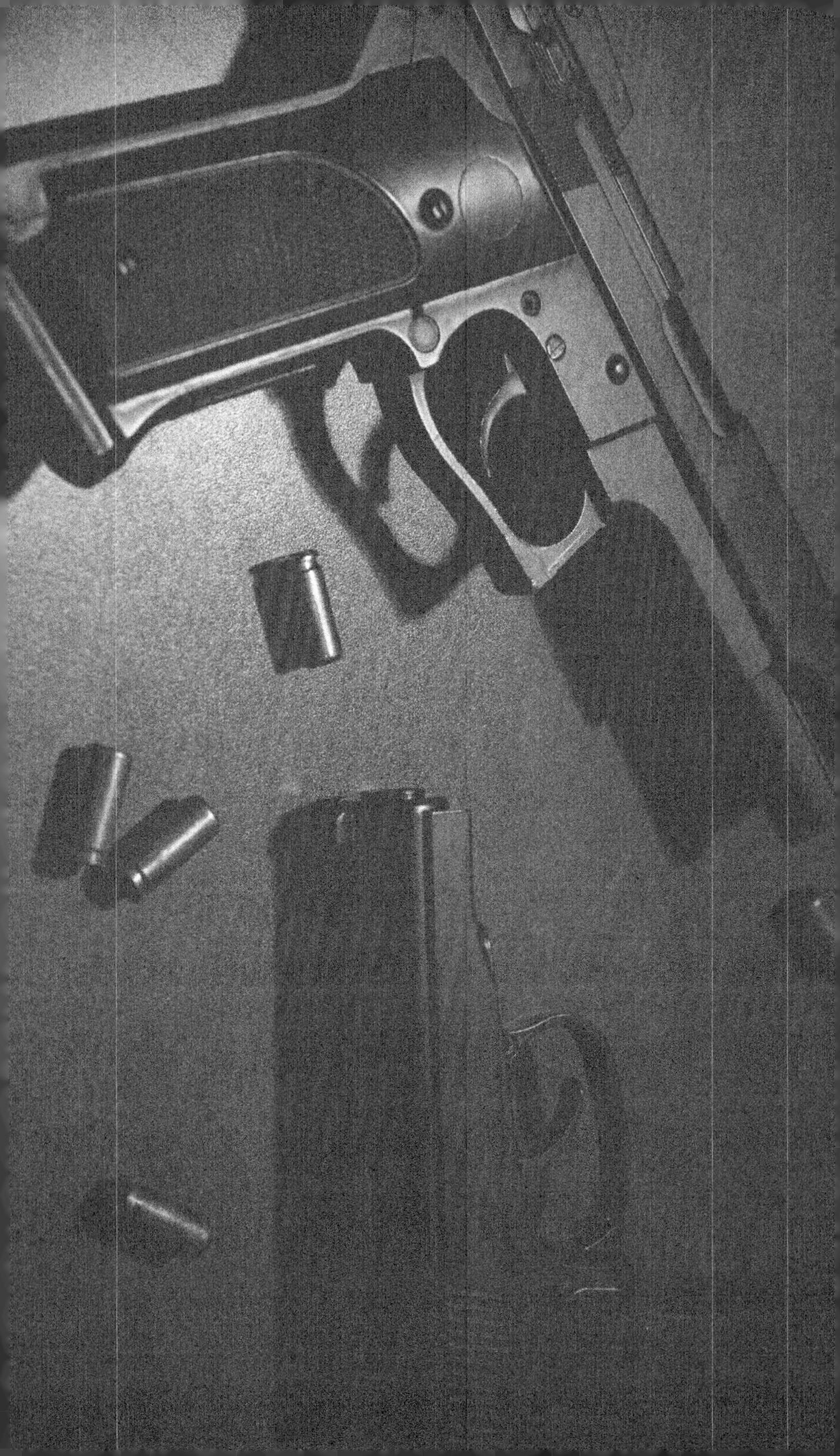

# Chapter Seven

## Viktor

As she stares up at me, something flickers over her face. I raise my eyebrow in question.

"He isn't my boyfriend," she says with confidence, leaning a little closer to me.

"I know." I grin as her eyebrows raise.

"How?"

I lean in, my cheek brushing against her soft one. "I have a way of knowing things." Mostly by doing background checks, which I admit, I can't wait for all of her information to come through. Impatience is a terrible trait.

She sucks in a breath, and I chuckle as I move away.

"Let's go back to your place," she mumbles, just loud enough for me to hear.

"Mine?" My lip tilts up. No chance.

"Yes," she says, rolling her shoulders back.

"What about yours?" I ask, knowing she lives alone.

"I live with my brother," she lies.

I grin. Oh, little doll, I'll find out *all* your secrets soon enough. I shrug. "Not tonight."

Her jaw drops, and I almost laugh at her pretty face in shock. I have other plans for her. Usually, I *would* bring her back and fuck her until she can't feel her legs, but she just lied to me. She is hiding something, and I intend to know more first. Liars don't get rewards like that.

She lifts her chin and smiles. Even though I rejected her. I'll be following her home anyway; she just doesn't know.

"Well, it was nice to meet you, Viktor." Then she passes by me. The other dancer, Damien, watches her leave and starts to follow her. I grab his arm before he reaches the door. "Stay away from her," I practically snarl.

His jaw visibly clenches. "Or what?"

I raise an eyebrow. "How much do you value those legs of yours?"

His face pales, and he backs away. I leave and set out to follow my little doll as she hurries out the door to see her other dancer friends.

I pull out my phone while I wait for her, texting Konstantin.

> Need more on Amaia. I want everything.

> On it. Will let you know what I find ASAP.

---

A small noise from upstairs pulls me from my thoughts as I close and lock her front door with a quiet click. I sneak towards the singular staircase and wait, avoiding the creaks that I located earlier.

Soft moans come from one of the rooms. I know she doesn't have anyone else here, as I've been out in the car for hours waiting for her to turn the lights off.

I walk up the stairs swiftly until I reach her bedroom door. She still seems to be asleep. A moan escapes her again, and I can't stop myself from entering the room. Looking over at her as she pants. She is having a sex dream. Dirty girl.

My fingers trail along the smooth, bare calf that is uncovered, up to the inside of her thigh. Stopping abruptly as she moves her hips toward me, searching for someone to give her a release. I brush my fingers over her tiny shorts covering her pussy. No panties, and she's soaked through.

It's so tempting to move them to the side and push my

fingers inside her. But tonight isn't about that. Reluctantly, I pull my hand away, holding onto my throbbing cock through my pants. I need a release.

Silently, I free my cock from my pants and stroke myself above her. Faster and faster as I imagine her writhing underneath me as I thrust my cock into her for the first time, knowing she's not dreaming of someone else fucking her.

Her pretty lips part slightly until a name threatens to spill. I want to hear her say mine. Her hand brushes over her nipple, and it pebbles under her tank top.

Fuck, I want to tie her to the bedposts and be inside her so bad. As I feel my orgasm building inside me, I fuck my hand harder, leaning closer and closer to her until I cum all over her shorts, straight over pussy. Marking my territory. I run my finger over my tip, where a tiny drop of cum sits. Using the same finger, I rub the small amount on her lower lip. When she wakes, she will taste me. And she will love it. I lift the bed sheets and cover her.

I'll have her one day. On my terms. But for now, I leave.

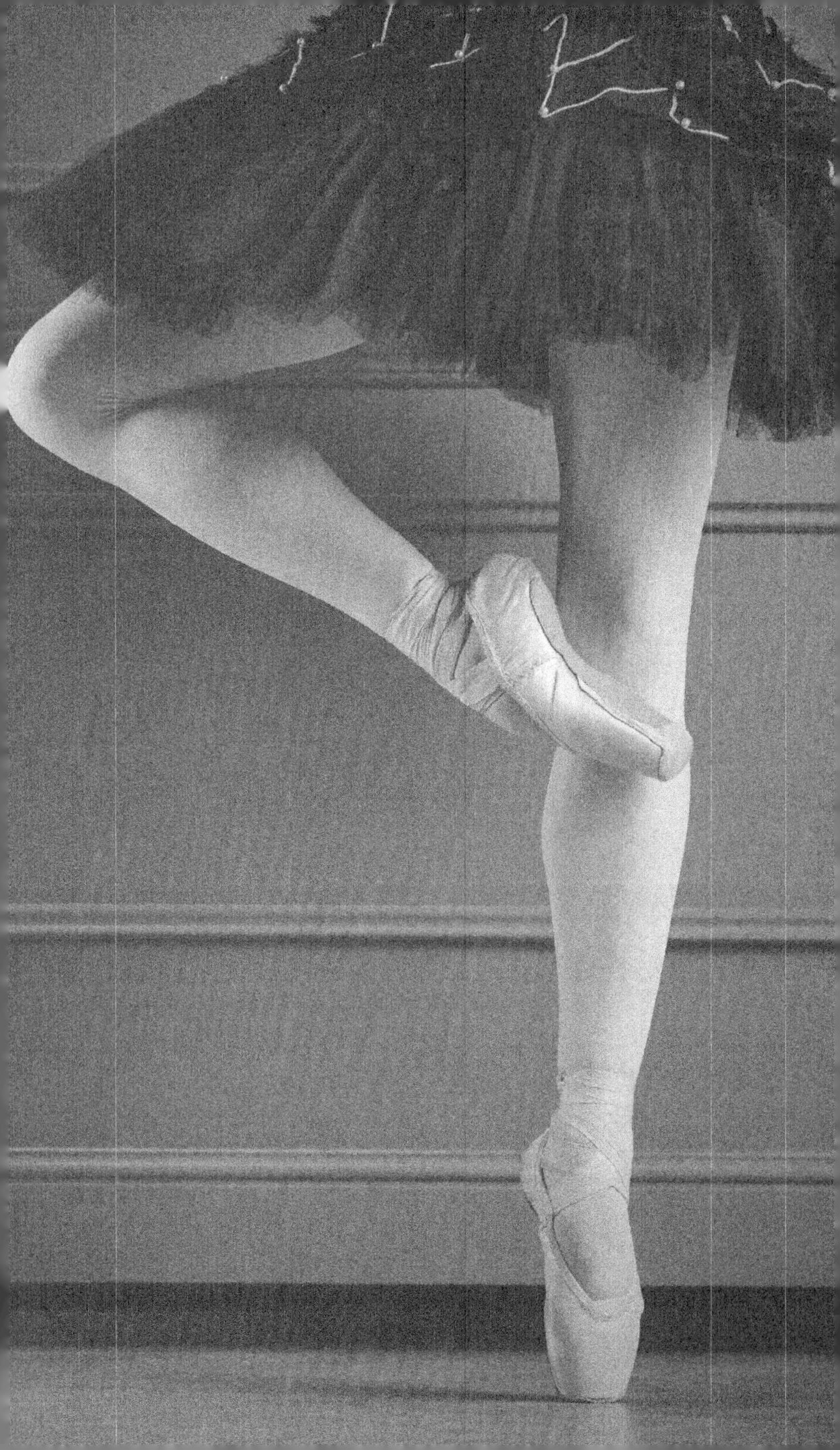

# Chapter Eight

# Amaia

I'm pulled from my sleep from my cell phone. I go to roll over to my front to hide away, but then realize my shorts are hardened in some places. What the fuck?

Ripping the sheets off me, I notice the white marks all over my clothes. Is that someone's cum? I run into the bathroom and rip the clothes from my body, not caring about waiting for the water to heat up. I squeal as the cold water shocks me awake.

Somebody was here, in my house.

My heart picks up pace, thumping with purpose against my ribcage. The water slowly turns warm, and I try to figure out who it could be. I'm pretty sure it was Viktor, but now, I'm not so sure. He doesn't know where I live.

But Damien does, and he has been extra touchy since Dmitri didn't turn up at my show.

I shut off my shower, yank the towel off the rail, and wrap myself up. Almost slipping on the tile as I storm out the bathroom, I pick up my phone from the bedside table to see texts from Damien. I ignore them and call instead.

"Hey, did you get my—"

"What the fuck. Were you in my house last night?" I can't help but raise my voice.

My now wet hair slaps me in the face as I lean down to pick up the cum-covered clothes between my fingers, holding them out in front of me to take them to the laundry hamper. I lay them on top and remind myself to do washing as soon as I hang up, my lips curling in disgust.

"No, why? Did something happen?" he asks, concern lacing his words.

"Someone was in my house!" I yell through the phone. He has a crush on me, but is he capable of breaking into my home?

Nausea rolls over me, and I drop the phone, running back in the bathroom and kneeling over my toilet, retching on my empty stomach.

I take deep breaths to stop my heart from hammering its way out of my chest. I run my hands through my tangled hair and stand over the sink until I calm my breathing. I just stare at myself. I need to think rationally.

A frantic knock at my front door pulls me away from

my reflection. I shove on some clean clothes as quickly as possible, nearly falling over as I struggle to yank on my jeans. I rush down the steps as the knocks become louder as whoever it is pounds harder.

"Open the door. Are you okay?" Damien's voice calls through the door just as I reach the bottom step. His fist pounds the door again. "If you don't say anything, I'm going to break the door down."

I rip the door open, almost off the hinges, and stare at him. He pushes through and holds onto me, squeezing. I freeze.

"I thought something happened. You said someone was here last night." He holds me back at arm's length, checking over me. I'm sure glad I put some full-coverage clothes on before opening the door. I can't stand the thought of someone seeing more of me while I'm feeling vulnerable.

"I'm fine, just thought someone was," I lie, but I'm pretty sure my voice just went a pitch higher than average.

Damien's eyes narrow, and he pushes past me.

I stop my fists from curling. "I'm okay, I promise." I regret mentioning someone being here now; I didn't think he would rush over or be this possessive. Now I need to get rid of him, needing to be alone.

"I'm just going to check around the house. I need to know you're safe," he calls out.

I sigh and leave him to wander around while pouring myself a glass of pineapple juice, rolling my eyes at how ridiculous this is. Damien can get too touchy, and I don't like it. He never takes the hint, no matter how hard I try. I shouldn't have opened the door.

"What the fuck is this?"

Shit, he's upstairs. If he's in my bedroom, he will see the cum-covered clothes. I place the glass on the table and run upstairs. Seeing him holding my shorts and top out away from his body almost makes me laugh. His nose wrinkles and he drops the fabric to the floor. I chew on my lower lip to stop myself from saying anything, but he just stares at me, waiting for an explanation.

"I spilled yogurt over myself when I fell asleep last night. Couldn't be bothered to change." Another lie. I'm always clean, and I wouldn't eat in bed either.

It's a shame he can read me.

"Do you need me to stay here, keep you safe?" He nudges the clothes away from him and steps into my personal space, but I back away, my ass bumping the dresser behind me. "I'll stay. You don't need to worry." He holds onto my shoulders, but I shrug him off.

"It's not necessary," I tell him, forcing a smile. Although, it doesn't feel genuine right now. I need him to leave.

"I'll just be on the couch. If anyone breaks in, I'll get to them first."

I don't tell him that I don't think he has any chance against my intruder if it's Viktor. He could snap Damien like a twig with those huge muscles of his. Damien has muscle, but Viktor looks like he would use his body for violence.

"I'll be fine. If I need you, I'll call." I emphasize the smile further, hoping to ease the rejection.

He huffs out a breath and looks away. "Fine. I need you to call at any sound," he says through a clenched jaw. He hugs me, and I try not to move, waiting for him to let go. It's a moment too long before he does.

I tuck my hair behind my ears. "Thank you for rushing here, but I've got it now. I'll see you later to train?" I open the door and practically throw him out.

Then I walk back into the kitchen for my juice, finding my glass is empty. My eyes flick around the room while I stand deathly still, expecting to hear something, anything. But it's silent. A shiver runs down my spine.

Was whoever it is here until just now?

My uniform is all packed, and I'm ready to go to training. Show Claudia that I'm not a complete disaster and don't need to be replaced in our next show. I can do this; I am capable of becoming Prima. I have been dancing since I was seven, and I was born for this.

I've gone through the stages of bloodied toes and aching positions until I perfected every movement I could possibly do. But I'm still not enough. Work harder. Never stop.

We spend thirty minutes on the barre, doing the basics before moving onto our own choreography. I choose to be by myself today so Damien can't offer to partner up with me. It seems awkward since this morning. I understand he is concerned, and so am I, but this is my mess.

My eyes glide along the other dancers, especially Charlotte, our current lead dancer. AKA my competitor. I watch her movements, knowing I'll need to be better than her. She's always seemed to be a little cold toward me, but I'm not sure why. Damien tells me to just leave it, that she must be jealous, so I should just ignore her. That I'm the better dancer.

But the more I watch her, the more I don't believe it. Not once has she made a mistake. Sometimes I wonder

# VIKTOR

how I'm going to beat her perfection.

Six hours later, I'm changing out of my uniform. I'm avoiding the showers here, as knowing that everyone can see my naked body somehow makes me nervous. I push the thoughts away for a moment while I think back to last night. Am I really safe? Surely, if Viktor wanted to hurt me, he would have by now?

I don't know what he wants. It's frustrating.

I groan as I hear the rain against the glass doors before I step outside. I can't help the sag in my shoulders. God hates me.

I make a run for my car down the street on my sore feet, pushing through the people with umbrellas because I stupidly didn't bring my own. Fall is usually warm here, with pretty views and barely any rain. But now, the weather matches my stressed mood.

When I reach the car, I stab the key into the door to get in as quickly as possible. And because of the day I've had, I check the back seat and lock my doors as soon as I'm inside to make sure I'm alone. Only then do I lean back and breathe.

Shaking my head to myself, I put the car into drive and pull out into traffic, checking the mirrors more than usual in case I see a car following me.

When I ease into my driveway, I check around all my neighbors' houses to see if anything seems out of the ordinary. New cars, or just anything strange. The windshield wipers and rain are making it hard to see anything.

But as far as I can tell, there's nothing amiss.

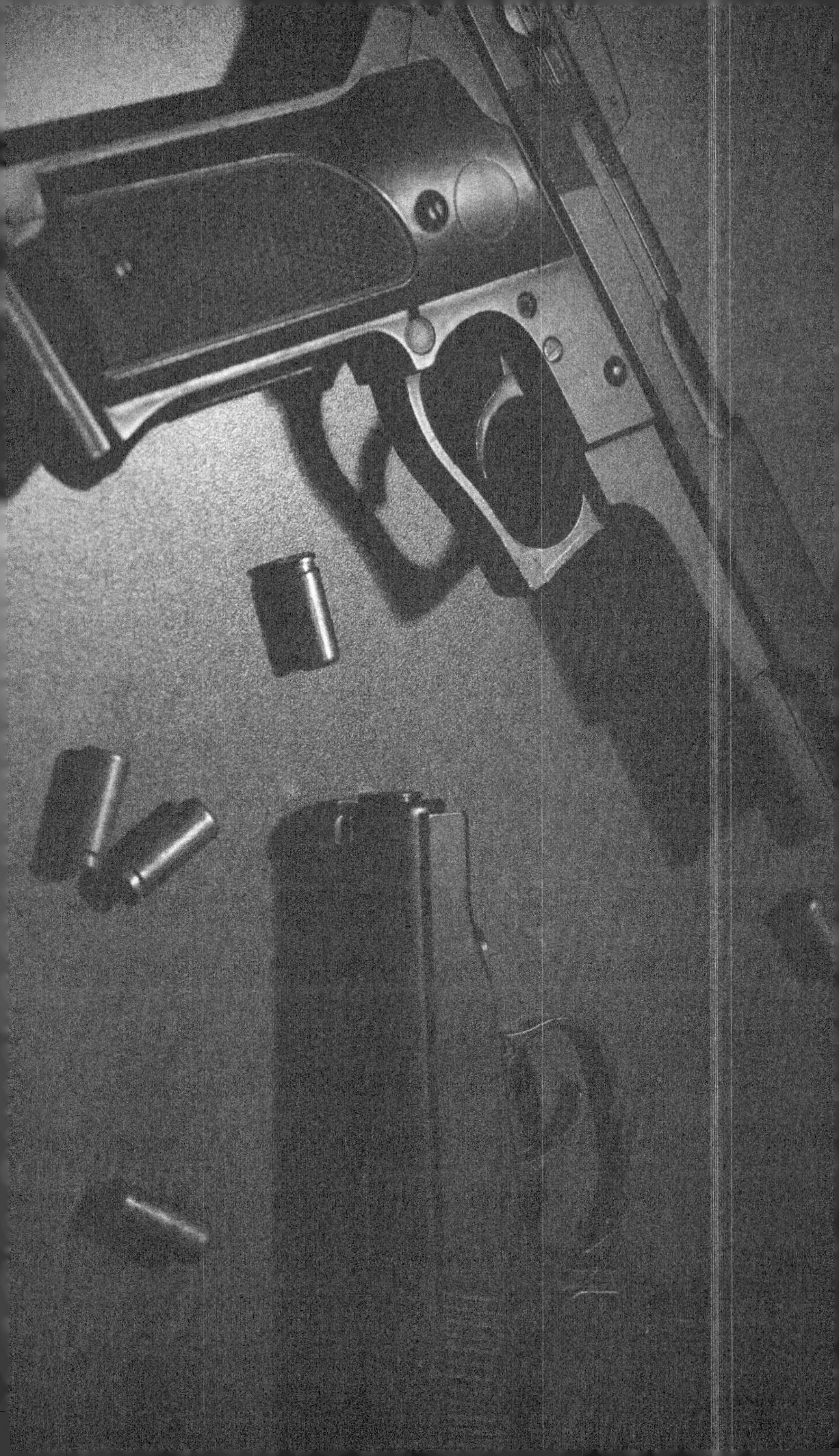

# Chapter Nine

## Viktor

It's dark in her home, the only sounds being the cars driving past me. But I want to find out what she's up to. I had already been inside, and her home doesn't have any personal touches except a couple of photos hanging on the wall. One that I found was of her as a young child with who I assume is her mother at a ballet performance, and they look alike. I place it back where it was and continue through the house. She seems like an only child, with an absent father. But why say she has a brother? So easily, too.

After I've found nothing in her home about a sibling, it makes me think of my family. Having four brothers it wasn't easy growing up in a big family. Especially after my mother was murdered.

My fists clench at the memory, rage boiling just beneath

the surface. My father did a great job with us over these last ten years, and we're all still close. He had asked us to run our own parts of the business outside of Chicago, which is where he lives now.

We're all going back for Christmas in a few months. It feels like I haven't seen them in forever.

We still protect each other no matter what, though. The loyalty of the Petrov family is unmatched. My fingers itch to call them, wanting to know if they are having problems with the Koskovich family and traitors, but I'm sure they would know.

---

Each night, I can't stay away from Amaia. Following her to make sure she's safe, watching over her while she sleeps. Wanting to touch her. Last night, I ran my fingers along her bare pussy.

The tip of my finger had entered her and wanted to go further, but I stopped myself. She isn't ready for me yet, so

I backed away.

After memorizing the layout of her home, I sat in the car, waiting for her to go to sleep like always. Now, I watch her through the windows. She walks out the steamy bathroom in a towel, clutching the top of it. She leaves the blinds open. But she must know she's being watched, sauntering around in a towel. She stands facing the wall where I know there is a full-length mirror and drops the only fabric hiding her little tight body. I nearly groan. Perfection.

She stares at herself for a moment before running her hands over her body as if she is inspecting herself. My brows furrow as she grabs at her skin on her lower stomach and pinches it. She drops her hands and shoves on some clothing, keeping her eyes on the floor.

My phone vibrates and I look down, seeing Konstantin's name flash.

"What did you find?" I ask as a greeting, knowing the reason he is calling's because he drudged something up on her.

"She has a brother, and you're not going to like who it

is," he says warily.

"Spit it out," I order, voice sharp.

"Her half-brother. It's Dmitri."

"Dmitri who?" Anger pulses through me.

"Koskovich."

I stay silent and seated in my car, taking in deep breaths to calm myself. No fucking way. "Boss?" Konstantin calls out through the speaker.

"I'll deal with it," I retort as I hang up. It's not until long after the lights go out that I make my way to the small door and step inside the darkness.

Now that I know who she really is, I need more.

I sneak into her bedroom with ease, seeing her smooth legs are twisted around the sheets. I peel them back so she is bared to me. I prefer her like this, quiet. But now, I need answers. Taking off my jacket and folding it over a chair, I place the duffel bag I keep in the trunk of every car I own on the vanity and pull out the rope.

Amaia stirs as I straddle her, the bed dipping beneath my weight. Grabbing her by the wrists, I pull them up and tie her to the headboard. Her eyes fly open just as I wrap the rope around her.

"What are you doing?" She thrusts her hips to get me

off, and I chuckle.

"Oh, little doll. I'm here to know why you lied to me, but keep moving like that and I'll get other ideas." I grind my hips against her, my hard cock rubbing against her core.

She shudders and damn do want to fuck her right now. But I need to focus.

I pinch her nipple. "Have you lied to me?" I ask, already aware that she has, I want to know if she'll admit it.

She stays silent, chest heaving. I flip her over, yank her shorts down, and spank her.

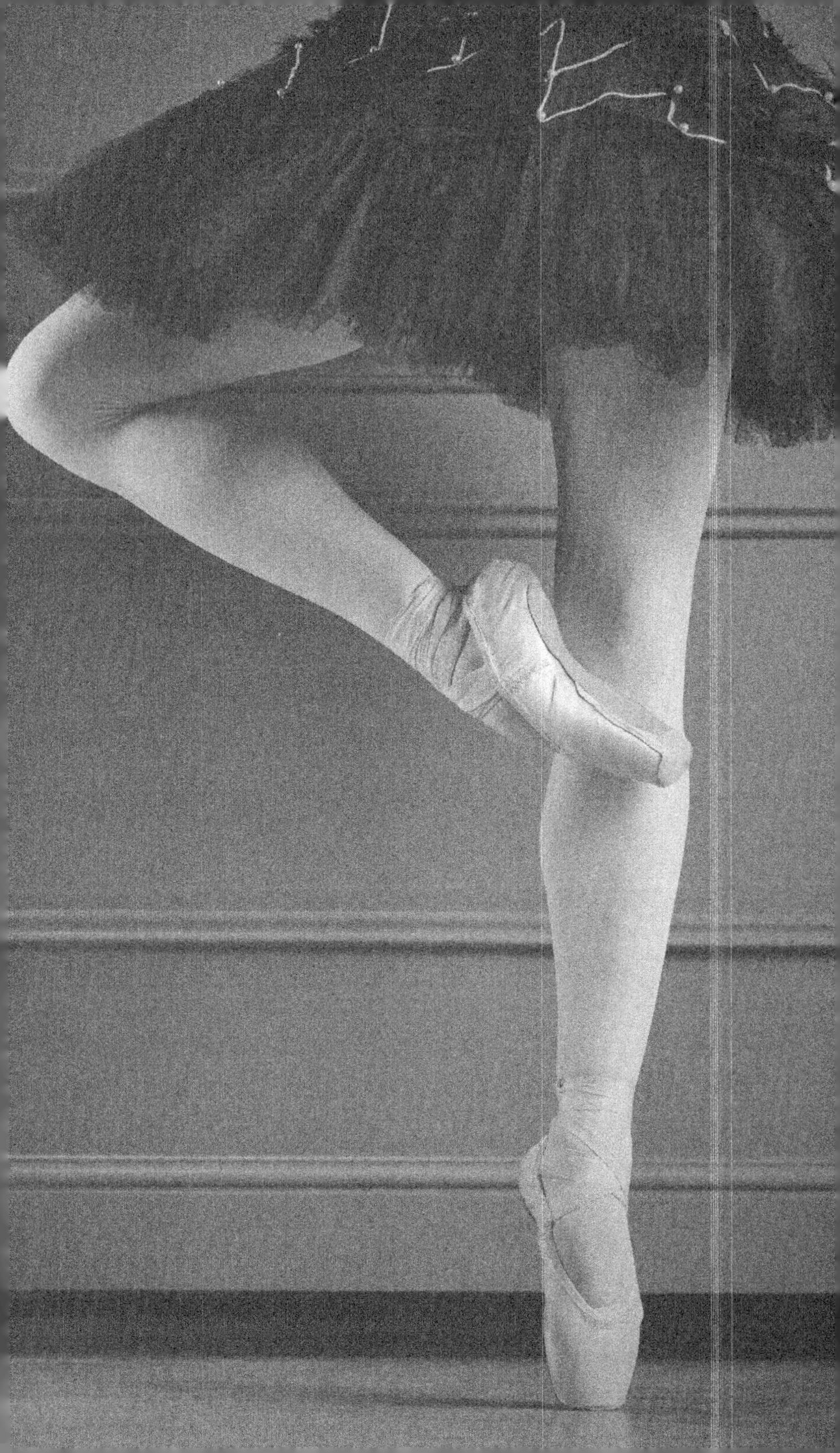

# Chapter Ten

## Amaia

"What's wrong with you?" I shout while yanking on the ropes. He's enjoying my struggle, his hard cock pressing into me, but my fight instinct is kicking in.

He pinches my nipple which had gone hard. "I thought you might like this," he says with a raised eyebrow. I glare at him.

"Koskovich, tell me what the name means to you," he orders.

I don't answer him, but fuck, I know how these things go. He will get his answers and kill me. It's best I say nothing, so my lips clamp shut.

He flips me over and pulls my shorts down; I wiggle more to get him off me. He lifts my hips up, and my shorts stay at my bent knee. The bed dips where he moves, and I scrunch my eyes shut. But the sharp sting of his hand on my ass pulls me out of my panic. He hasn't moved behind me, so that's good.

"Be a good girl for me. Tell me what you know about Dmitri and the people he works with."

But I don't know anything about the men he keeps around; my head lolls side to side as tears fill my eyes.

He spanks me again. "I know you're not fully related."

I cry out as he spanks me one more time but leaves his hand resting on what I assume is now a handprint. He gently rubs on it as though to soothe any pain. It makes me melt, and I relax. Surprisingly, being tied up and spanked is relaxing. Not to mention I can feel myself getting wet. Something inside me must be broken.

My current position shouldn't be turning me on.

"We have the same dad; I'm an affair baby. My dad is Russian, and my mom is an American and left to raise me alone. Dmitri reached out a year ago; he knew I existed somehow. He protects me. I don't know where he is, I promise." The words all rush out at once. I'm hoping he will untie me and leave. Kind of.

Another part of me wants him to get behind me and force his cock inside me. Oh shit, am I unlocking kinks?

Viktor's nose runs along my body. Is he smelling me? I try to shift to look but can't. My head doesn't stretch that far around. He moves behind me and pushes my upper back into the bed and spreads my legs. My heart beats hard inside my chest.

His hot, wet tongue glides from my clit to my asshole. I still, not knowing what to do.

"You taste just as I thought you would," he mumbles into my ear.

Then he stands abruptly, leaving me on the bed. I twist around and notice he is grabbing his jacket and a duffel bag. He pulls a knife from his pocket. My eyes widen, and I try to move away, but the ropes are too tight. Viktor chuckles and cuts my bindings.

"You need to relax more. I'll teach you in time," he says as he walks out the door while I'm still rubbing my sore wrists.

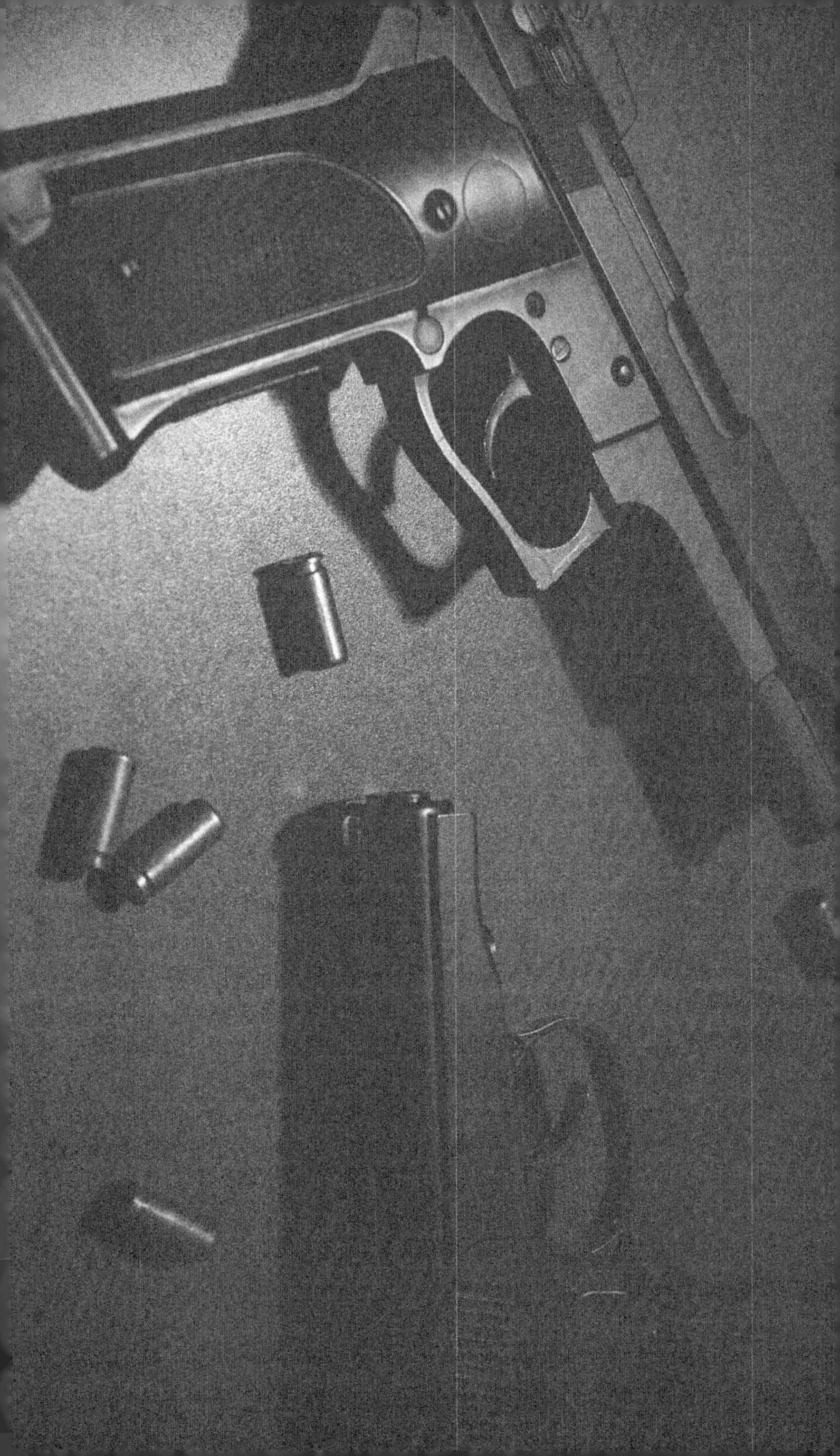

# Chapter Eleven

## Viktor

I couldn't help myself last night. Tying Amaia up, I had to use it to my advantage. The spanking was for answers. But her facial expressions showed me she was enjoying it, with her eyes dark and lips parting for me. I don't think she even realized it when a moan slipped through.

She wanted it. I just had to know what she tasted like, and I knew she'd be wet for me. She just isn't used to being tied up; I don't think she knows what she truly likes. I'll need to ease her in.

I park my car at the warehouse, where a couple of my guards wait outside the large metal door. I press the numbers on the keypad and unlock it. It opens and the creak gains everyone's attention. Dmitri is tied to the chair in the middle of the spacious room inside, head hanging down and piss covering his pants.

The door slams closed behind me and echoes through the large empty space. The only things in the open area are the large rusted beams spread throughout and scattered dirt along the ground. Konstantin steps beside me, holding out a pair of leather gloves. I put them on and clench my fists. With a grin, I stand in front of Dmitri, who tries to back away, but being tied to the chair makes it difficult. Out of pity, I squat in front of him. The stench of his unwashed body almost making me gag.

I tilt my head as he lifts his pale face, still avoiding eye contact. "Hello, traitor," I start.

He peers at me through narrowed eyes.

"I'm just returning things back to their natural order," he spits, quite brave for a man bound and under the watch of several armed men. It's possible he has resigned himself to knowing he will die whether he speaks to me or not.

I sigh. "Bring in the chair," I call out without taking my eyes off Dmitri. Fear flashes across his features, but he straightens his back.

Two of my guards bring in a large wooden box and open it. The iron chair. I always had a thing for medieval torture; after all, they always did seem to get results. But the chair?

It was slow and painful. One of my proudest inventions.

"No, you can't do this!" Dmitri struggles within his restraints.

Konstantin steps up by my side.

When I cut open the ropes that bind him, he goes to attack me, but I'm prepared and punch him in the ribs, breaking one of them. He bends at the waist, clutching his side.

We drag him over while he screams in protest. But I don't listen. We strap him in the chair and the small iron spikes all over that dig into his skin. We keep him strapped down by the wrists and ankles with another across his chest.

"Do you have anything to tell me yet?" I ask, raising my eyebrow.

He spits at my feet. "I'll never tell you anything."

I reach out to one of the guards, who passes me a wrench, and I tighten his straps just enough to draw blood. He stills, seeming to realize that the more he moves, the worse it is for him.

I chuckle. This is just the beginning.

"Maybe you will talk if I bring your sister in, sitting opposite you. In a similar chair." I smile suggestively, knowing I have him. The words taste like ash in my mouth, but I know her name will get him to talk.

He laughs, surprising me. "I don't have a sister." He wiggles a little more but curses the chair, and the spikes go deeper into his skin.

I lean in until we are face to face. "Amaia disagrees with you."

Dmitri's face goes two shades whiter than I thought was possible.

"How did you find her?" he yells.

I circle the iron chair like a wolf about to tear apart his prey, the steps of my shoes echoing in the silent warehouse.

He sneers, "Don't touch her."

It's sweet that he cares.

I lean down, my head next to his ear. "I'll take *very* good care of her," I chuckle.

His face turns red as he struggles, blood seeping from his tiny wounds. But he pushes through it. I wanted to keep him here for days, in this chair as he slowly loses his will to live.

"My Uncle Yuri is alive, that's all I know. Stay away from Amaia," he rushes out. But I only shake my head. "There is more, and you know what it is. Could it be your father? We haven't seen Ivan lately. Were you stealing from me for him, stealing my clients? Which lost me and my family money, need I remind you. You didn't just do it for your Uncle. This is for power, and I want the list of all involved and where they are. Then I will make sure Amaia stays safe."

Dmitri clenches his jaw and stares holes at the ground. I move back in front of him and tilt my head, waiting for everything to be spilled.

They want their power back. The Koskovich more than hate us for taking everything from them; the arranged marriage wasn't fair. He has to be my little bitch at work as a drug runner. I pull my Glock out from the holster and smack him round the face.

"You think losing my mother even compares to losing power? Maybe I should take Amaia, fuck her, and slit her throat just as she cums all over my cock?" My rage is building inside me like an inferno about to burst. I need to let it all out.

Dmitri shrinks back as much as possible. I stand straight and seethe. Without taking my eyes off him in front of me, I pass the gun to Konstantin.

"Undo the straps," I order, shucking off my jacket.

The guards do as I command and force Dmitri out the chair. He lands face-down on the floor with a cry. Little bloodied dots cover his back, arms, and legs. It's not as satisfying to see as it would be to put each hole in individually by hand.

"Get up," I say with deadly calm.

He pushes himself up with shaky, weak arms. I don't give him time to stand before kicking him in the face. His jaw cracks in the silent room, and a couple of teeth fly out his now bloody mouth, scattering across the dirty floor.

Still, I'm not satisfied.

I lean over him and grab the front of his shirt. My fist pounds into his face, over and over. Blood sprays over my arms and face. I don't care. His face caves in, and still I don't stop. I can't stop. The rage consumes me.

This is for my family. For my mother.

A hand grabs my wrist before I punch Dmitri's smashed-in face again. I take a deep breath and look up at

Konstantin. He doesn't say a word, but I stand.

Dmitri's been dead a while, and now he doesn't even have a face.

"Send his body as a message to the rest of them."

A chorus of "Yes, boss," echoes through the warehouse as I storm back to my car, screeching away from the scene.

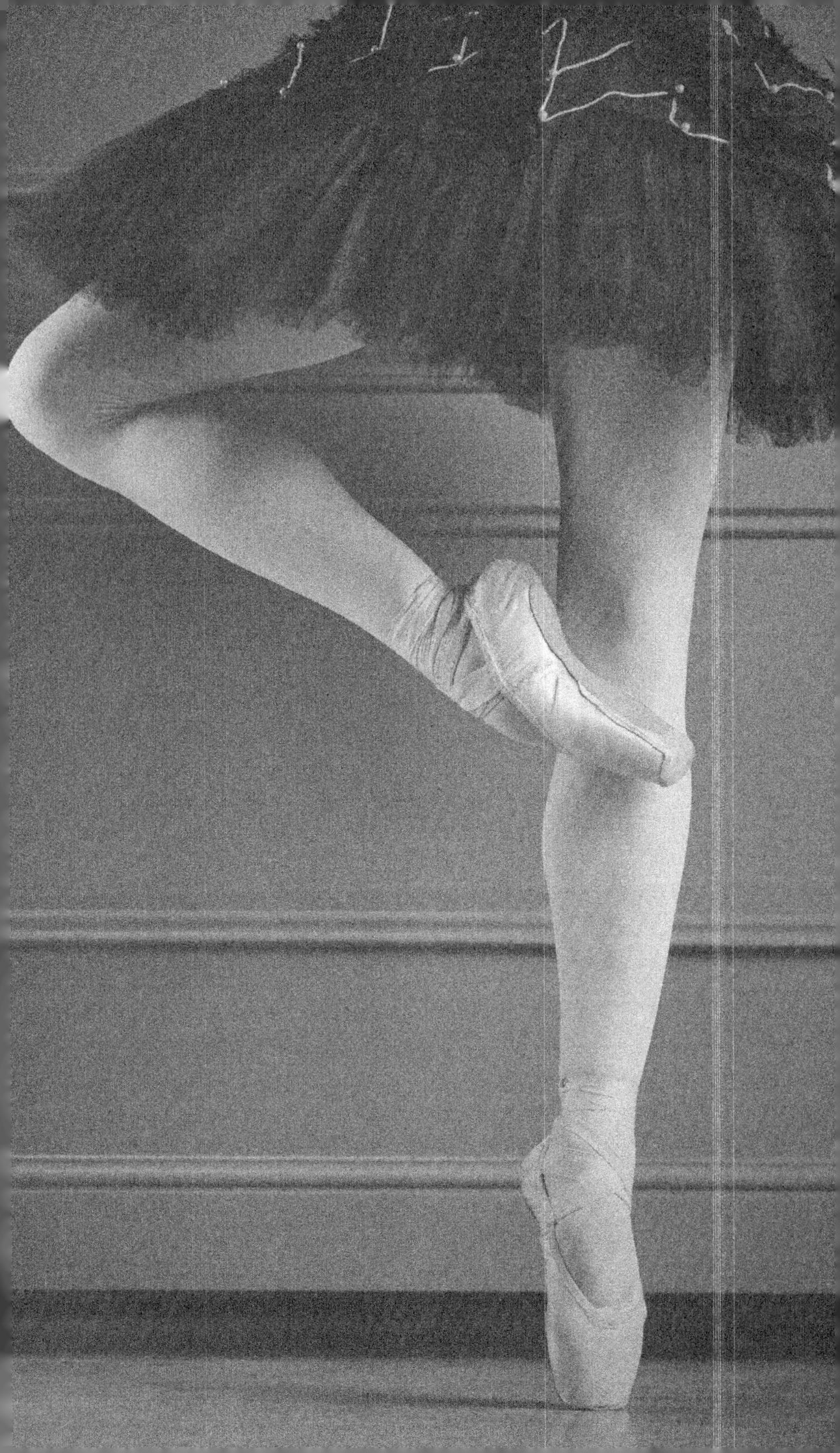

# Chapter Twelve

## Amaia

I step inside my house, turn off my new alarm system, and lean against the door, an audible thunk of my head dropping on the surface. It's nice to be home.

Until I open my eyes.

Wet footprints show a man's size-shoe disappearing up the stairs. It had been a few days, so of course he would be back.

I place my dance bag on the ground and sneak to the kitchen, my eyes darting around, staying silent and listening for anything. I grab a knife and hold it out in front of me, trying to keep my hand from shaking. I know I need to go upstairs, make sure he isn't here. But what do I do if he is? Can I stab him? I want to. But can I? Is it in me to protect myself to that extent?

I should run outside or call someone. But I'm tempted

to know more. It's like that old saying 'curiosity killed the cat' even though it might even be true this time.

I'll risk it; I'm too damn nosy for my own good.

Edging my way across the wall, I follow the footsteps leading into my bedroom. He better not be going through my panty drawer like the pervert I know he is.

Turning the corner, I see Viktor relaxing on my bed with his ankles crossed and hands behind his head. Dirty shoes over my nice white satin sheets. I lift the knife up as he turns to me, and he chuckles.

Viktor drawls, "Hello, little doll. I've been waiting for you."

"How did you get in?" My heart is beating fast. I try not to think about how good his hair looks while it's wet and hanging down over his forehead or how his eyes are glimmering with amusement. Or how his suit fits him perfectly, the wet shirt showing every inch of muscle.

Our gaze locks again. My eyes narrow as he smirks; it's as though he can read me.

"Does it matter how I got in, or why?" he wonders.

I swallow. "Both," I retort, my voice trembling.

"It's easy to get in." He shrugs. "And why? That's the true question, isn't it?"

I can't stop my eyeroll. "Don't be cryptic. Why are you

here?"

He takes off his jacket, the white shirt sticking to his pecks from where the rain had got to him. *Stop staring*, I scold myself.

"I'm here because I can't stay away, even though you have Koskovich blood running through your veins." He shakes his head, tsking.

I take a step back, and he moves toward me, but I hit the doorframe with force, momentarily knocking the wind from me.

He fists my hair, yanking it back to stare at him. I lick my lips, and his eyes zero in on the gesture. He grabs my hand with the knife in it and pins it against the wall, his body pressing up against me as the knife falls from my grip.

I'm trembling for a whole other reason now.

"What are you thinking about, little doll? You're all flushed." He smiles like a wolf who just found his prey. My brows furrow. Am I enjoying this? Why am I heating up?

"Not you," I say in a breathy whisper, the lie flowing easily from my mouth.

He leans in, kissing me on the jaw; it's so light I wouldn't have noticed if my skin wasn't so hyperfocused on his touch.

"Have you ever just given into your desires? Let go of control? Given it to someone else?" he murmurs against my skin.

*Please don't touch me and see how much I'm enjoying this.*

But it's all too much. I've never given into my desires, but fuck it. I know it will happen one day. He makes me feel things I never thought existed. I hate that he can.

Viktor smirks, like he knows my thoughts. Cocky bastard. His hand slides up my leggings and rubs small circles over my clit. My eyes flutter shut at the sensations coursing through me. He pushes in a finger, and I can't stop myself from grinding onto his hand while resting my free hand rests on his chest.

He lets my hand go moments later, and I give in. I rip open his shirt; the buttons scattering along the floor is the only other sound in the room other than my heart thundering inside my chest. Oh my God, he is perfection beneath this fabric, the artwork painted along his skin and muscular body.

Oh gosh, is that a 'V' in his muscles? I've never seen that in real life before. His tailored clothes didn't do him justice. My mouth goes dry. Can I really do this?

"What are you waiting for, little doll?" His husky voice roams over me, and I feel my panties soaking, I need them off. He unbuckles his belt, steps back while taking off the rest of his clothes, and nods toward my outfit. "Get undressed, on your knees, and crawl to me."

For some reason, I obey. I never like being told what to do, but his voice. The demanding tone. I'd do anything right now. He drops his pants and boxers. I can't stop my jaw from dropping.

My eyes roam over his godlike form before I slowly crawl over to him until my mouth is so close to his cock and his fingers run through my hair. I stare at him, my eyes wide. Should have known he was well hung and fuck me, piercings line all the way up his cock.

"What is that?" I ask, staring down at his hardness in wonder.

"It's a Jacob's ladder, little doll. Think you can take all of me?" He chuckles, and it's as though he is sensing my inner turmoil. I lick along his length from the base to the tip, my tongue going over each ridge.

"Easy, you're not that big," I mumble, but as I move my mouth over him, I only manage to get halfway, proving myself wrong.

His hand tightens in my hair and pushes me down further, making me gag on it, praying he doesn't keep pushing. I watch him through my lashes, and my eyes water as he hits the back of my throat. Each of the barbells of the piercing brushes against my tongue.

The more I suck, the more he moans, and I'm loving the noises he makes. The salty taste of precum is on my tongue, and I slowly suck until I reach his tip, and he pops out my mouth. He grabs my arm and yanks me up until my feet are off the ground.

He leans back on my bed, pulling me on top of his body and grabbing hold of my thighs, pulling them to either side of his hips so I'm straddling him.

"Your tits are the perfect size," he groans as he massages them.

Thoughts flood my mind of who he is and how much he hates my family, so I lean over and fist the handle of the pen knife from under my pillow that I had been keeping there since he last came in here and hold it to his throat. He smiles, but I hesitate.

"Oh, you like it kinky." He flips me over and settles between my legs, pinning my hands above my head. The knife clatters to the floor.

Viktor lines himself against my pussy as I struggle to move. He forces himself into me, and I cry out. "Are you working with your brother?"

I swallow down my panic as he wraps his hand around my throat, squeezing me slightly. My body is on fire, the stretch of him burning inside me with the sensation of the piercings is different; I'm almost begging him to move, but he refuses until I give an answer.

"No, I don't get involved with his business," I manage to get out over the feel of him deep inside me.

He grabs my chin and forces me to look into his eyes. My pussy clenches at how much danger I seem to have got myself into. But I can't stop the images rolling through my mind of him fucking me, so close to ending me, just like I wanted to end him.

*There is definitely something wrong with me.*

"What do you mean, little doll?" he asks, tightening his already bruising grip around my wrists, but something shines in his eyes. Is that pride? What the fuck for? I'm confused.

He slowly pulls out of me, but my legs tighten around him.

"Let's not ruin the mood. Tell me you want this," he says, not moving another inch.

I don't say anything. He nips along my jawline until he's hovering over my lips. So close together, if I just moved forward a millimeter...

Viktor whispers, "Tell me to stop and I will."

I don't say a word. Every single warning in my head is short-circuiting, and nothing is coming out my mouth.

He takes the opportunity to kiss me, tasting of vodka and sin.

He forces himself back inside, moving his hips while my eyes roll to the back of my head. He moves my legs over his shoulders, forcing himself deeper. I swear he is touching somewhere that has never been touched before. My back arches into him, and his mouth latches on to my nipple. The moan that falls from my mouth sounds a lot like his name.

"That's it, little doll, scream my name."

A sharp pain comes from my shoulder where he bites down into my flesh. My eyes open, and my blood has spread across his lower lip as he continues pounding into me. My lips part, and he kisses me again.

He kisses me how he fucks me, and I forget my own name.

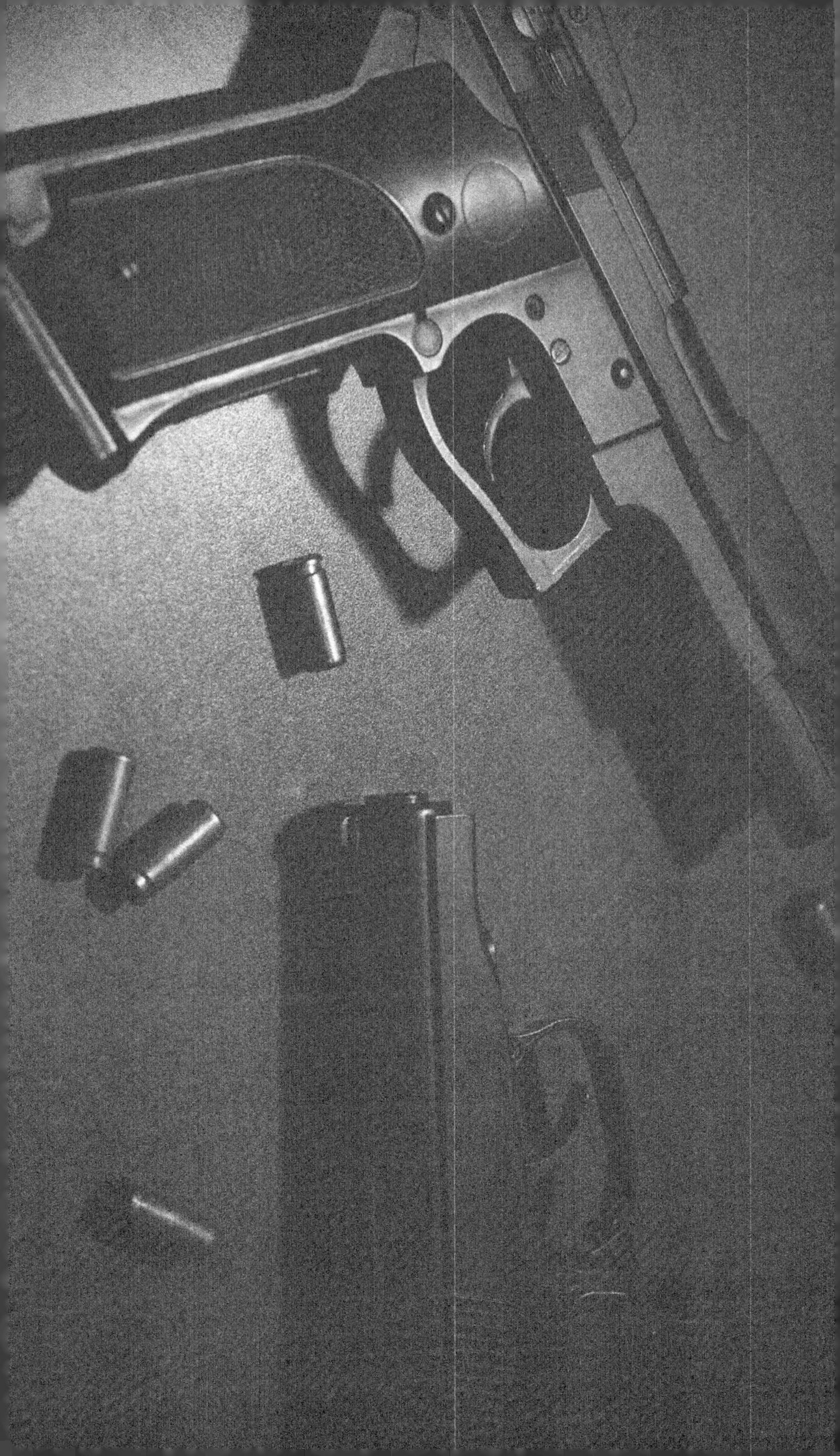

# Chapter Thirteen

## Viktor

Her tight little pussy strangles my cock, the pulsing of her inner walls as she comes hard. It drags out my own orgasm. It's the hardest I've come in a long time. And I'm deep inside this tiny ballerina who wanted to stab me and damn it, I want it again. Including the attempted throat slitting. That was exciting. I hope she does it again.

"Told you that you'd be screaming my name, little doll." I chuckle while still balls deep inside her. I let go of her arms and let her legs down.

A sharp sting spreads across my cheek. "You're an asshole!" she yells as she pushes me from the bed. She doesn't have a lot of strength, so I move off anyway, and she rolls off the bed from under me.

"Yes, I am." I shrug as I move to sit up, she struggles to walk. But tries to hide it, albeit unsuccessfully.

She squeals in frustration before she reaches her closet,

quickly covering herself with her robe, leaving it loose on her body. She leans against her closet door.

"You came inside me." She gestures to my cum dripping down her thigh.

I step into her personal space, run my finger through it, and shove it in her mouth. "Taste me."

She gags as I force my fingers down her throat.

If looks could kill, I'd be dead right now.

"I hope you're on the pill." I move away to grab my boxers and shove them on, walking out of the bedroom to grab a drink like I belong here.

She storms after me, her feet light on the wooden floor like the little dancer that she is. I raise an eyebrow at her. She tightens the robe and holds the knife up to me once more. She looks good with the 'just been fucked' hair. I'd like to see it again.

"Why do men always assume women are on birth control?" She waves the knife in my direction.

"Because women usually are. I did say to you that you can tell me to stop. You knew I wasn't wearing a condom, so I guess you need to take care of it." I shrug, her nostrils flare, she is furious. She throws the knife at me, and it misses. Feisty.

"Fuck you," she seethes.

"I'd rather fuck you. Give me ten minutes and I'll be

good to go again," I retort, helping myself to a bottle of water I know she keeps in the fridge. I try not to frown at the lack of food inside.

She storms over and shoves my bare chest, but I don't budge.

"You are infuriating," she huffs, hair falling in front of her eye. I tuck the strands behind her ear.

"And you're acting like I didn't just give you the best orgasm of your life. Get over it, little doll."

She pushes me again, and I raise my eyebrow at her feeble attempt.

"That wasn't the best orgasm of my life." She crosses her arms over her chest and lifts her chin.

"I'll have to try again then." I smirk, and her cheeks blush. Next time, I'll make sure she can't get out of bed.

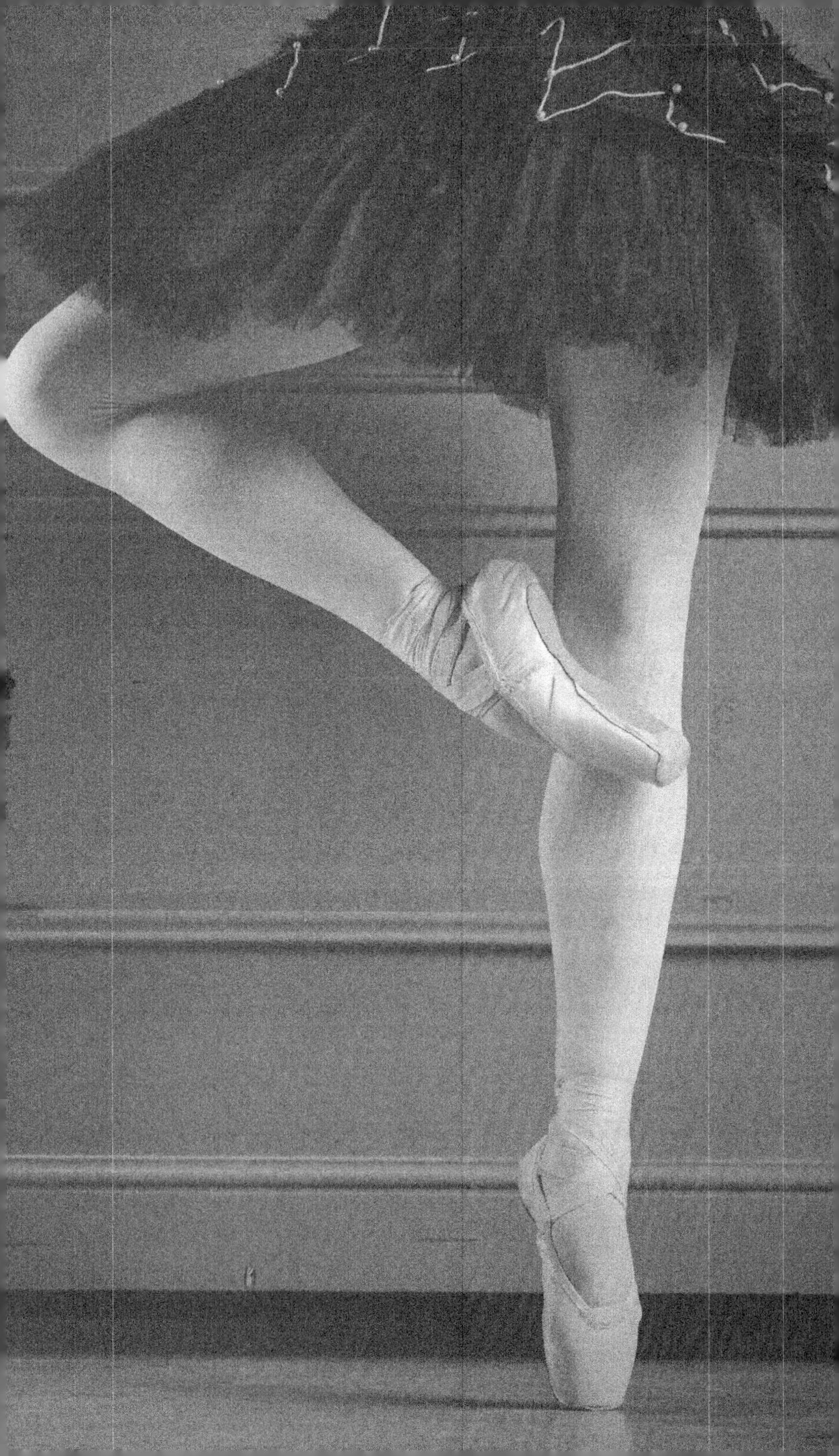

# Chapter Fourteen

# Amaia

I didn't sleep last night after I made Viktor leave. He was reluctant but promised he would be back soon. I'm not quite sure how I feel about that. Viktor inside me was intense; I couldn't get him out of my mind for hours. The memory of how different it felt, so deep, and the piercings made him touch everywhere. I was only able to stand from adrenaline.

I had given him control of my body, and he took care of me. I've always had to be on the lookout for myself, controlling my emotions. My mom always told me I have my dad's temper and I should dance through it, forcing it deep down until I choreograph my own personal dance.

I wouldn't know about my dad's life or much of who he is. I'm just an affair baby. Even though he used to call me his little princess, when he did visit us anyway. He must have been too busy with his *real* family.

Stepping into the studio early, I'm glad no one is here yet. I need the extra training since I fucked up before. Even though I'm still feeling sore, I need to push through it.

My career is important to me, and time is passing too quickly before I can become Prima. My one and only dream since I found out what one was. I'm hoping the early morning will show Claudia how committed I am. I look down at my body in disgust, mentally adding, *Maybe if I lose a few pounds too.*

Changing into my outfit, I notice the bite mark on my shoulder is still visible. Fucking Viktor. I pull the straps of my leotard on further, hoping to hide what it is, but the girls walk in the changing room.

Beth, another girl who is currently in the running to get Prima status, stares at my new mark and scrunches up her nose. I narrow my eyes at her, childish I know, and walk out with my head held high. My ears catch the word 'whore,' though. Snickers follow me just as the door closes. Damien walks out the opposite changing room just as I do, and his eyes glide down my body. I turn before he can judge me for the bite mark too. I'm going to kill Viktor.

I step up to the barre and begin stretching out my legs. Stay in control.

"Leg higher, Amaia," Claudia calls out as she walks closer. I clench my jaw; I fucking would if my vagina wasn't pounded by a huge cock last night.

I breathe through each movement. Plie, tendue, pirouettes.

Damien offers to be my partner for the combining leaps. We have partnered up before many times, but he seems to be acting differently today. He has always been so careful, but now his fingers graze across my nipple or his hand a little too close between my legs.

I can't imagine how Viktor would feel about this, but also I shouldn't really care. This is just dancing, as it always has been.

Once our dance finishes, I back away quickly, suddenly feeling uncomfortable.

"Do you want to grab dinner after this?" Damien asks with a smile.

I paste on my own fake smile and apologize, "I've got plans tonight." Not many people know, but I have a key to the studio so I can practice in the evenings, many extra hours in fact. Especially now that the shows are over and we have a few weeks' break. I can't miss any spare moment of practice.

"What are you doing?" Damien asks, stepping closer to me and placing his palm on my shoulder.

I bite the inside of my cheek, and a slight metallic taste fills my mouth where I'm pressing too hard.

His eyes narrow in on the mark on my shoulder. "Are you sleeping with someone?" He roughly grabs me and pulls me closer.

"That's none of your business," I tell him, hiding the trembling in my voice.

He lets out a humorless laugh and shakes his head.

"We could have been good together, you know that." He steps away and turns toward the changing room. I know I've hurt him, but he knows we would never happen, and my sex life is none of his business.

A bad feeling settles in my gut, and I rush into the bathroom and lock the door, keeping my ear against it, waiting for everyone's voices to go. Including Damien's. Especially his.

Once everyone has left, including Claudia, I plug in my phone and play my favorite song to dance to and get lost in the movements.

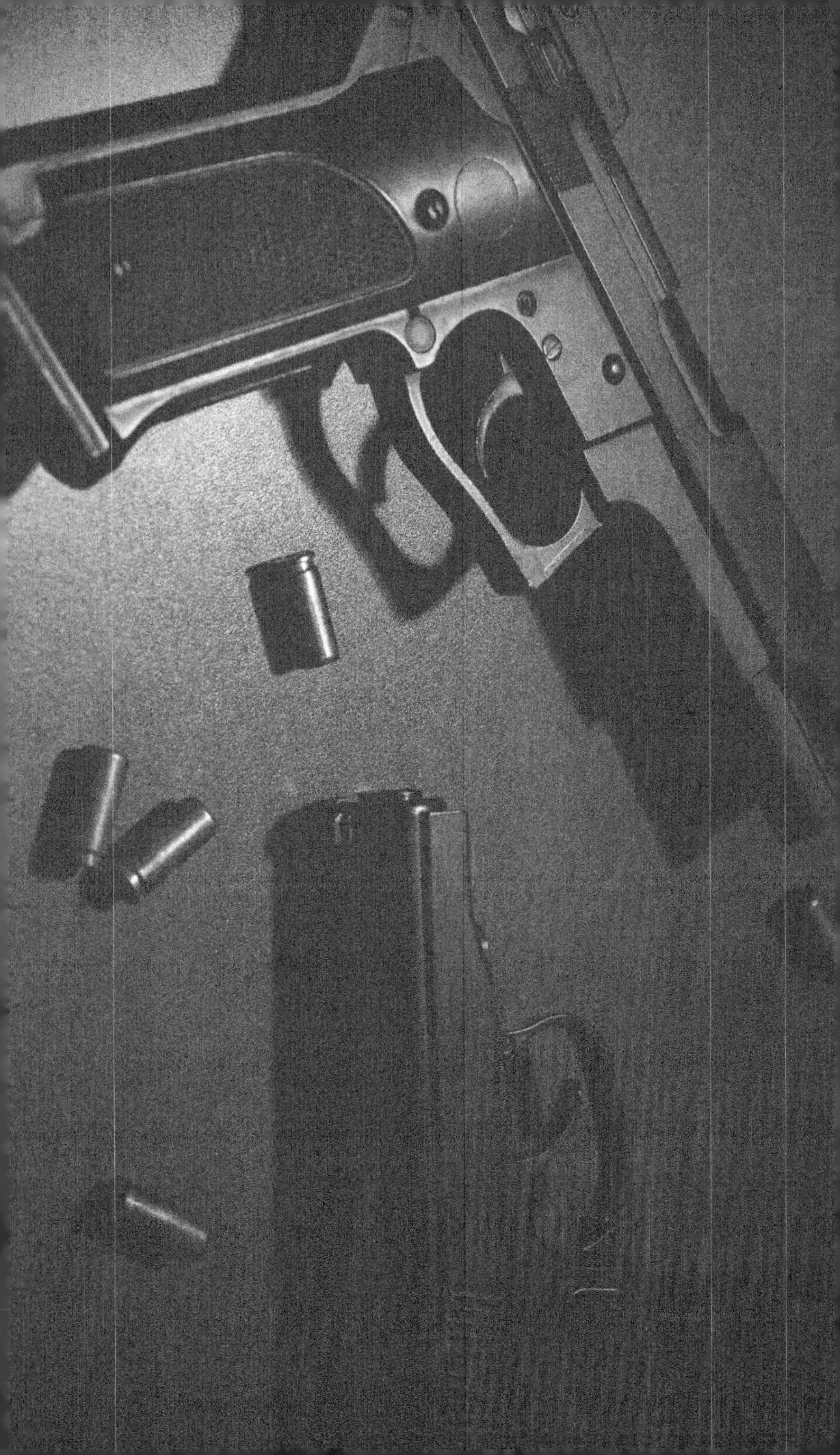

# Chapter Fifteen

## Viktor

She can't see me as she spins on her toes, elegance radiating from her. I lick my lips, remembering how she writhed beneath me. The need to taste her pushes one foot in front of the other.

She doesn't look at me; I think she's too lost in the moment as the music flows through her. I need this. I need her calm.

The phone call I received earlier confirmed that Ivan is alive, but I don't know whether he will come for Amaia, whether it's to keep her safe from my family or to use her as a bargaining chip. People know of my old reputation.

The song hits the crescendo, and when she floats back down from the high, her eyes open. I grin as she glares at me. I'll never tire of her attitude, or anything about her. It drives me crazy. I adjust my pants as I begin to harden.

She storms over to her iPhone and turns the music off. I don't believe that she's angry at me but rather herself for wanting me. Enjoying what I give her. But maybe that's my ego.

"Please don't stop on my account. I was enjoying the show. You are so… bendy. My mind drifts to filthy places."

"You're disgusting."

She goes to move past me, but I pin her up against the wall. She doesn't fight me this time. Interesting.

My eyes drift down to her heaving chest. The little bite mark I left on her shoulder is clearly showing where her clothes have fallen down. I move closer and trace around the marks with my tongue.

"People saw that today and had questions. What the fuck did you think you would get out of this? Branding me?" Her nostrils flare.

I lean in until our faces are a mere inch apart. "I can leave my mark on you or break that bastard's legs. You decide." She needs to realize there is no escape from me.

And at this, she stays silent.

"So, what's it going to be, little doll?" I raise an eyebrow in question, waiting for her to answer.

"I'm debating," she mutters and rolls her eyes.

I press myself up against her body, my cock hard as steel and craving to be inside her warmth once more. She gasps when she feels me. Her eyes flutter closed as she lifts her chin as though she's searching for my lips. I don't give them to her.

I spin her around and hold her against my chest, her ass grinding up against me. Her body wants me, she just refuses to believe it.

"I'm bringing you back to my place tonight. I've got something to show you," I tell her, not letting go.

She hums and agrees, but I don't think she really understands the implications of what I'm saying. Or maybe she has realized that I'll just tie her up and take her anyway.

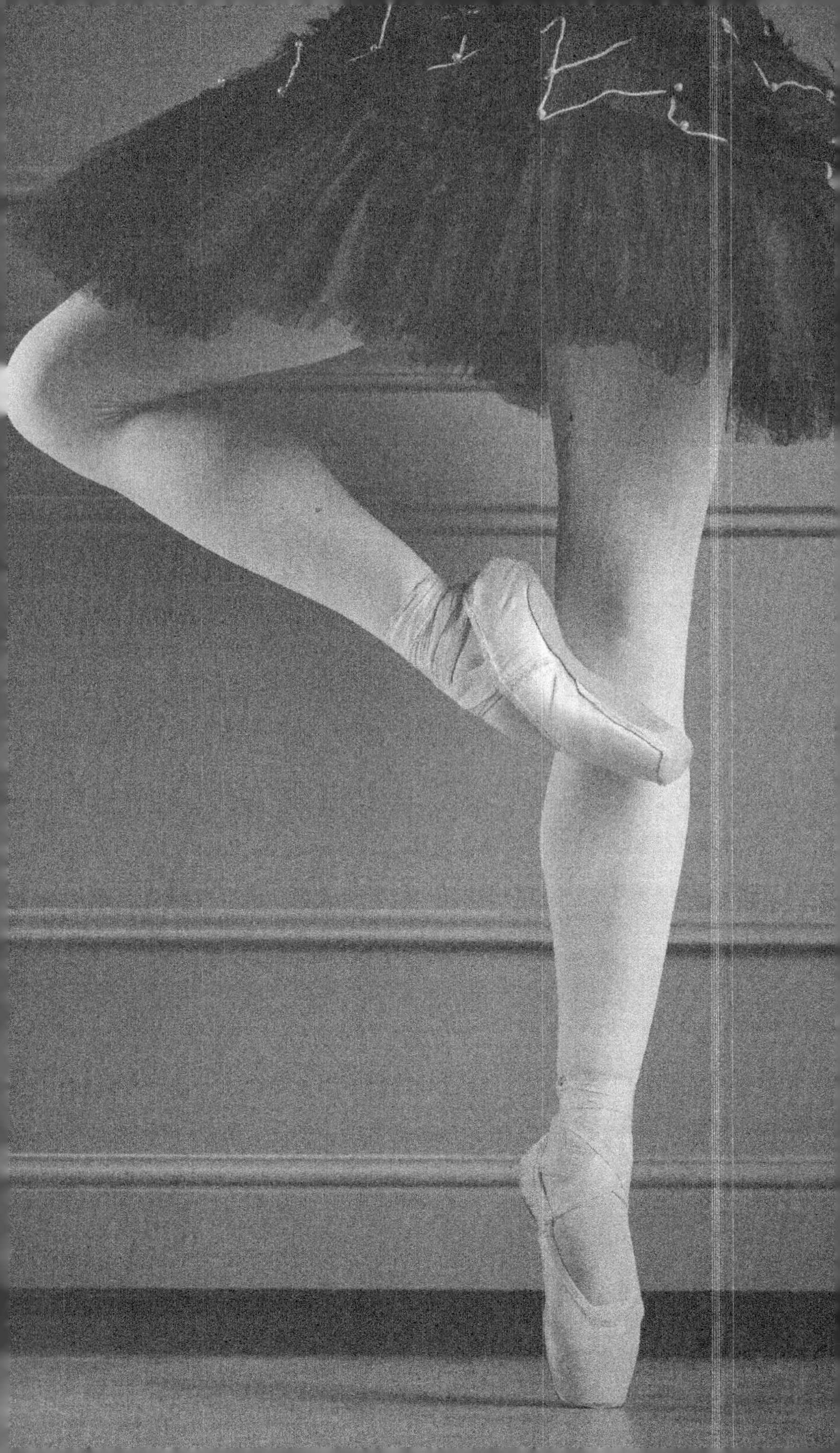

# Chapter Sixteen

# Amaia

I don't care anymore. He will do what he wants anyway.

He picks me up and takes me to the barre near the mirror, flipping me around.

"What are you doing?" I try to wiggling free from his grasp, but he's too strong for me. I keep fighting. We are in front of the mirror, and I only ever look at myself here when I need to, when I'm perfecting my form.

I squeeze my eyes shut. I don't want to see how imperfect I look.

I'm crushed against Viktor's body as he pulls me to his chest; I can feel every muscle against my back.

"Look at us," he whispers in my ear, his hot breath spreading to the sensitive spot on my neck.

I feel his hand slowly wrapping itself around my throat, and he squeezes.

"Look at how perfect my hand looks around you, the perfect necklace. Only mine, understand?"

He releases the pressure but doesn't move his hand, and my eyes peel open. I see myself, and I hate it. My hair is loose, my cheeks are pink, and I can see every lump on my body. I'm a mess. I avert my gaze to the large, tattooed hand still wrapped around my throat. His other hand glides down my body, and I wince because I know he can feel the pouch around my belly, but he squeezes again, and I can't breathe.

He lifts my dress and rips at the tights. Pulling my underwear to the side, he starts pressing small circles over my clit. My eyes roll to the back of my head. How does he make this so good?

"You're already wet for me," Viktor drawls.

My cheeks heat at the sight of him wrapped around me, the warmth of his body protecting me. I can't stop myself from whimpering when one hand leaves my neck and his other stops playing with my clit.

He reaches for his belt and takes it off, wrapping it around my wrists and strapping me to the barre. Moving me around like a little doll. I yank my arms, but I'm bound too tight. His fingers roughly push back inside me, pumping in and out until the only noise is my panting as he builds my orgasm. But then he stops, and a whimper rips from my throat.

"Not yet, little doll," he tsks.

A small thud echoes in the room, and a large hand presses my lower back until I'm bent over and I'm on my toes. I turn to the mirror to watch him as he lines up his cock to push inside me.

Each ridge of his piercings painfully push through me. He forces the last few inches, and I gasp. My head tips back, and his hand goes back to my neck as he fucks me, long strokes moving languidly inside me.

"I need your body as much as I need to breathe right now," he mumbles into my back.

I groan. It feels so good to be wanted, to be craved.

He pounds harder, my cries echoing in the studio. This is something I never imagined I would do. Not here, especially not being tied down by a stranger from the Mafia.

He slows down just as I'm about to come. "Please let me," I beg.

"Only if you watch yourself."

I hesitate, but the need to come takes over so badly that I watch us both, *just for a moment*. My eyes mostly stay on his face, the violence in the movement as he enjoys my body.

"You're mine," he growls, and I moan. Being with Viktor is the first time I've ever felt free.

I'm his possession and obsession and damn, it feels good.

His teeth sink into my shoulder again, and the sting sends shockwaves through my body. A coil tightens in my stomach and I come, my pussy pulsing around his cock, "Oh my God," I cry out as the aftershocks take over.

His thrusts speed up as he chases his own release and with a roar of his own, he floods me. Fuck, no condom. Again.

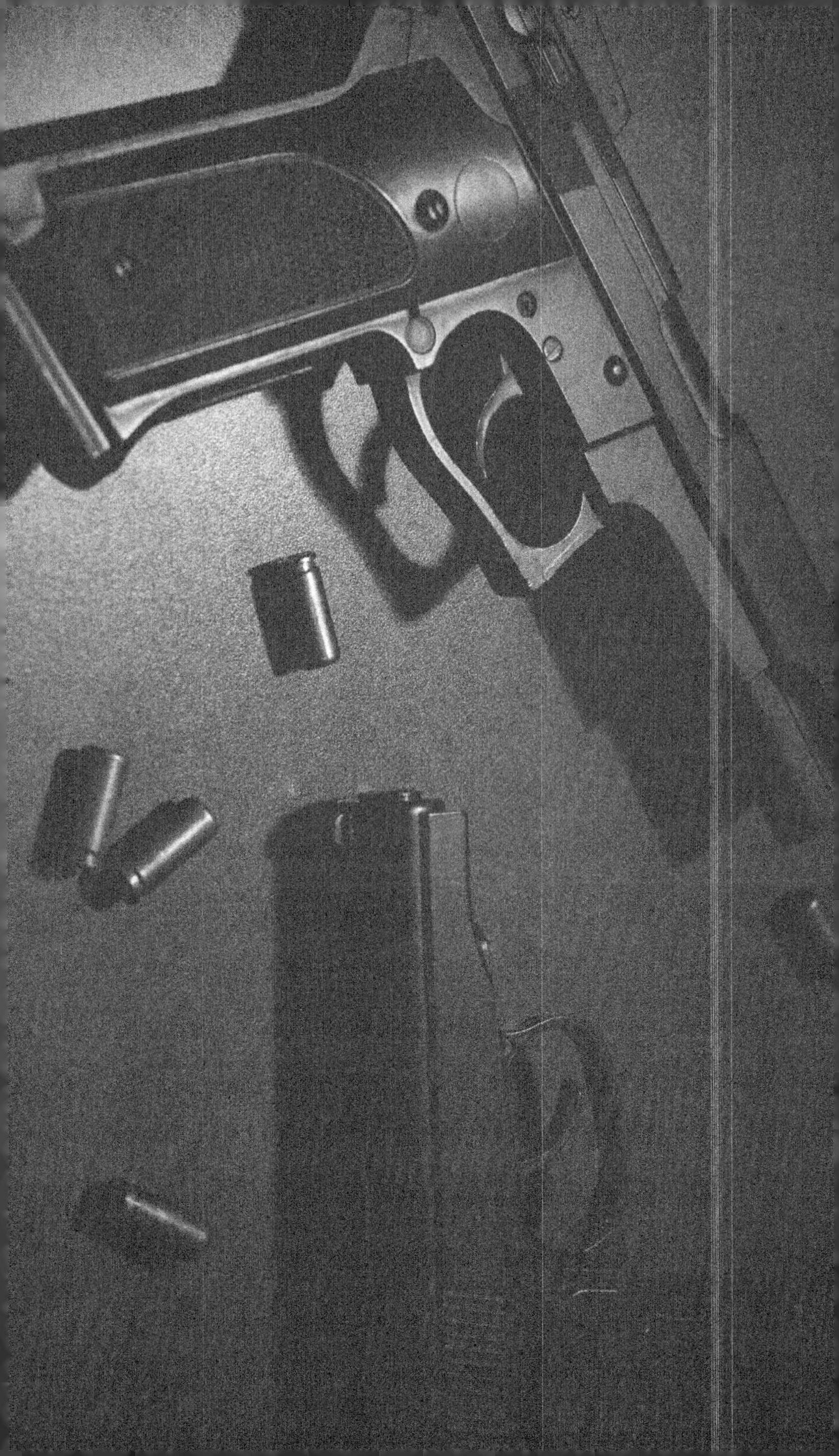

# Chapter Seventeen

# Viktor

I've known for a while from watching her that she hates her body. Tonight, I forced her to deal with it. She is perfection, and I want her to see what I do.

I've picked up on little things by watching her: She skips meals and barely looks in the mirror, and when she does, she grabs body parts and there's this look on her face. A look of self-hatred. She always cries after looking too long.

I don't believe she is too big or too small. I want her the way she is. So I'm taking her to my place, making sure she eats and knows her worth. I have installed a large mirror above my bed so that when I fuck her, she can see herself. Watch how beautiful her face is when she comes.

I pull out of her, and she sags in my arms with a content look on her face. "Let's go. My car is waiting," I say as I release her arms from being strapped by my belt.

"Waiting for what?" she asks, her eyebrows dipping in the middle.

"You're coming with me."

She pulls away, but I grab her body and hoist her over my shoulder. I push open the glass door and let it slam shut behind me. I walk us across the parking lot surrounded by bushes until I reach my car and lock her in the backseat. I quickly run back inside to grab her bag and phone from the changing rooms, and shove them in the trunk.

I need control, and she needs to let go. I'm taking her to my master room.

She is silent the whole journey with her arms crossed against her chest as she stares out the window.

As we get closer to my home and palm trees surround us with the setting sun casting oranges and pinks across the sky, her lips part, and she leans closer to the window. "You live in Beverly Hills? Isn't this a celebrity area?" she asks as we pass by the houses that get bigger

I shrug. "I like the houses. I didn't really want an estate, just a flashy home, and I work with celebrities sometimes anyway. It's convenient."

She turns to me with wide eyes. "You work with them?"

I grin but don't say anything; their discretion is what they expect of me. Quick deals and silence. Maybe she will learn one day, if I keep her around.

We drive up the mountainside and I press a button in my car, and the large iron gates awaiting us open. I pull around the large circular driveway, past the patios and park in front of the double brown garage door. "Home sweet home," I murmur and slip out the car. I rush around to open the door for Amaia like the gentleman my mother taught me to be. She ignores my outreached hand and climbs out herself, then crosses her arms across her chest.

"So, what did you want me here for?" she asks as I place my lower hand on her back and guide her to the illuminated steps to my house. Passing by the water features and we stand in front of the frosted glass door. I push it open and wait for her to pass into the foyer. Her eyes widen as she takes in the wide space. Her heels tapping along the marble floors as she approaches my unused grand piano. I step up next to her.

"I want to show you something of mine, show you something about me," I tell her. I don't look at her reaction. I don't want her knowing how much she affects me. People don't usually get close, or else they get hurt. But for some reason, I still want to show her this room that not many people know about. Get her to trust me. I gesture toward the curved staircase. She hesitates, so I hold out my hand, ready for her to take and we ascend them together. She's in awe when she looks out the windows at the view of the mountains.

"It's a beautiful view isn't it?" I ask, she turns to me.

"It's surreal. How did you get a place like this?"

I chuckle, "money, lots of it. I'll show you the outside soon. It's even better." I rest my hand on her lower back and guide her further up. We pass my office and game room.

We soon arrive at the closed door, and I press the numbers in on the keypad, waiting for the green light to flash. For a moment, I wait, watching her expressions as she takes in my space. She takes a sharp intake of breath, it's barely audible under the thumping of my heart. When I guide her inside, her head moves around, and I try to imagine seeing my playroom for the first time. Floggers lining the walls, restraints on the bed, and various toys set out.

She turns back to me as the door closes and I can't help myself, I press her up against the wall, my body against hers. Pinning her hands above her head, I kiss her. She moans into my mouth, and I pull back.

"Tell me how bad you want me right now," I whisper, pressing small kisses against her jawline.

"What?" she breathes out.

I grind myself against her, eliciting a gasp from her mouth. My lips curve into a knowing smile. Purely wicked.

"Tell me you want to try something new with me. You can choose the safe word." I wait for her answer as she looks around. Biting her lip, I can see in her eyes that she is thinking about saying yes.

Her head moves up and down as much as possible in our position.

"I need your words, Amaia," I growl.

Her eyes connect with mine. "I want this. I want you."

"Safe word?" I ask, reminding her how important this will be for us.

She licks her lip, mulling over her answer. "Red?"

"Perfect," I tell her, letting her go and holding onto her jaw before leaning in and kissing her deeply and roughly. We devour each other. Her hips grind against me, both of us completely lost in our moment.

I tighten my grip on her jaw, keeping her pinned to the wall. Then I trace along her neck with my tongue, teasing her senses. Her pulse speeds up as my tongue glides over it.

I grab her clothes at the front and tear through the fabric down the middle.

Eventually, I rip myself away, and she lurches forward to follow.

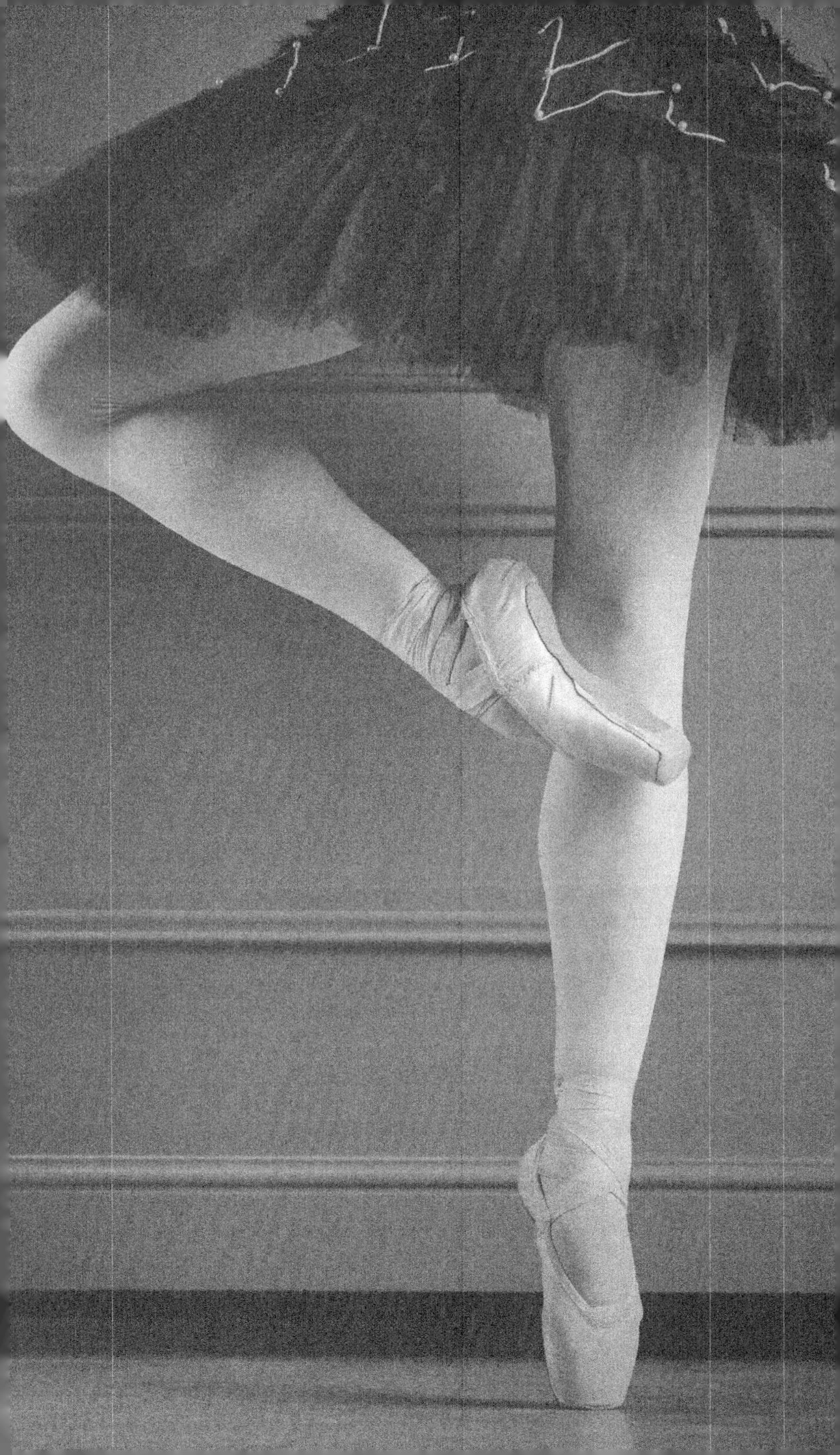

# Chapter Eighteen

# Amaia

He just ripped my clothes. Oh my God, I've never felt this hot in my entire life. The things he is making me feel... Oh no, I can't fall for a guy like him. *This is just passion*, I tell myself. I'm pulled back from my thoughts as every bit of clothing I was wearing is now on the floor. I reach out to unbutton his shirt, but I don't get the chance.

Viktor lifts me over his shoulder and throws me on the bed. I bounce in the middle. He moves over me, crawling up across my body.

That's when I notice he is holding something, a red silk scarf. I stare at him intently as he brings it over my eyes, tying it around the back of my head. The world goes dark, and all my senses are heightened.

"Relax, little doll. I'm going to take care of you," he whispers as he moves off the bed.

The sound of chains comes from next to me and before I know it, my wrists are pulled over my head, and I can't move far. He has restrained me to what I assume is the headboard.

Even though I can't see him looking, I feel the burn of his gaze trailing down my body. I'm vulnerable, exposed, and surprisingly wet like this.

"You're so fucking beautiful," he coos.

I don't say anything. Then his footsteps get further away until I hear the clink of ice cubes in a glass.

"I'm thirsty, are you?" he asks teasingly, and the smell of vodka fills my nose when he puts his mouth against mine. He slips away, and the bed dips at the end by my feet.

He grabs my left ankle and places an icy kiss on the inside. A gasp escapes me, but I quickly try to cover it up. He chuckles and continues to place those kisses along the inner side of my calf right up to my knee. When he stops, so does my breathing. My body is on fire despite the ice, desire running through me.

Next, I feel his cold tongue swirling around my nipple. My back arches, and he takes it in his mouth, sucking on it. His hand, cold from the glass, kneads my other breast before moving slowly down, tracing the sides of my body.

His fingers stop just above my pussy. "Do you want me to keep going?" His voice is raspy, and my body tingles.

"Please," I beg. I'm throbbing more than I thought I would be, and his ice fingers are the perfect contrast to my overheating flesh.

He rubs against my clit in small circles, then he sinks his fingers inside me. I gasp, not realizing he had moved until his cold mouth sucks on my clit. His fingers curl and rub against my g-spot. It doesn't take long until I explode, wave after wave of pleasure racing through my body.

He climbs on top of me and undoes the scarf, brushing his thumb against my cheek. "Are you okay? Do you want to keep going?"

"Please don't stop," I breathe out.

He hovers over me and stares into my eyes. "Remember your safe word. Tell me what it is."

"Red," I say as I move my hips up, searching for the part of him I need right now as he rips off his shirt and tosses it to the floor.

Unbuckling his belt, he curses in a string of Russian, impatience written on his face. Finally, after what feels like a long time, he thrusts into me, each piercing touching a different part of me. I'll never get enough.

He moans into my neck, "I'm not going easy on you, remember that."

I don't get to respond as he starts thrusting into me—hard. I can't touch him, I can't kiss him. He fucks me like a man who can't get enough. The headboard slams against the wall to the rhythm of his thrusts. I wrap my legs around him, encouraging him to go deeper. My next orgasm builds quickly, and I tighten my legs.

"Don't come yet," he demands, but I can't stop it; it's too late.

The tsunami of pleasure crashes over me again, and I swear my soul leaves my body for a moment. He picks up speed, and the only sound in the room is skin slapping against skin.

"Fuck," he groans as he fills me with his warm cum. He leans down and kisses me gently. "I'm going to punish you for coming without my permission."

I bite back a smile.

He reaches up and unlocks the chains, then pulls out

and rubs around my shoulders, easing the ache I didn't know I had. Viktor lifts me up and carries me to a bathroom I hadn't noticed before. Sitting me down on the edge of a counter, he turns the shower on.

Once the room is steamy, he lifts me into the shower and joins me. Washing me, caring for me. Making me feel worshiped.

After we are dry, he takes me into his real bedroom and sits me on his bed. He passes me a steaming mug: hot chocolate. That's when it hits me that we are not alone in this house. I feel my face burning and I stare back into the mug. A staff member must have brought it.

"The room is soundproof, so try not to worry. Now drink that so I can take care of you."

I do as he says, attempting to push the thoughts from my head about the calories I'm consuming as he massages my thighs. I give him the empty mug with a small smile and without taking his eyes off me, he places it on the nightstand.

Then he squirts some moisturizer in his hand and starts kneading the rest of my body with expert precision. I moan; it feels so good.

"Your piercings, did they hurt?" I ask quietly.

He thinks for a moment before answering, "Everyone

has their own pain threshold. Mine's high. Do you enjoy them?"

I bite my lip, and he leans into me. "It feels different. Good different. I didn't know that piercing was even a thing."

He kisses the spot behind my ear. "As long as you enjoy it. I aim to please." He smiles against my skin, and I feel tingly all over. I can't say anything else. I merely relax in his presence.

Viktor massages me for half an hour and then brushes my hair. I'm surprised when he gives me a shirt to wear and puts me in his bed. I can't hide my smile. Tonight was a new experience, and I can't wait to try more with him.

He lies next to me and pulls me to his chest, kissing me on the forehead. "Sleep well, little doll."

I contentedly drift off in his warmth.

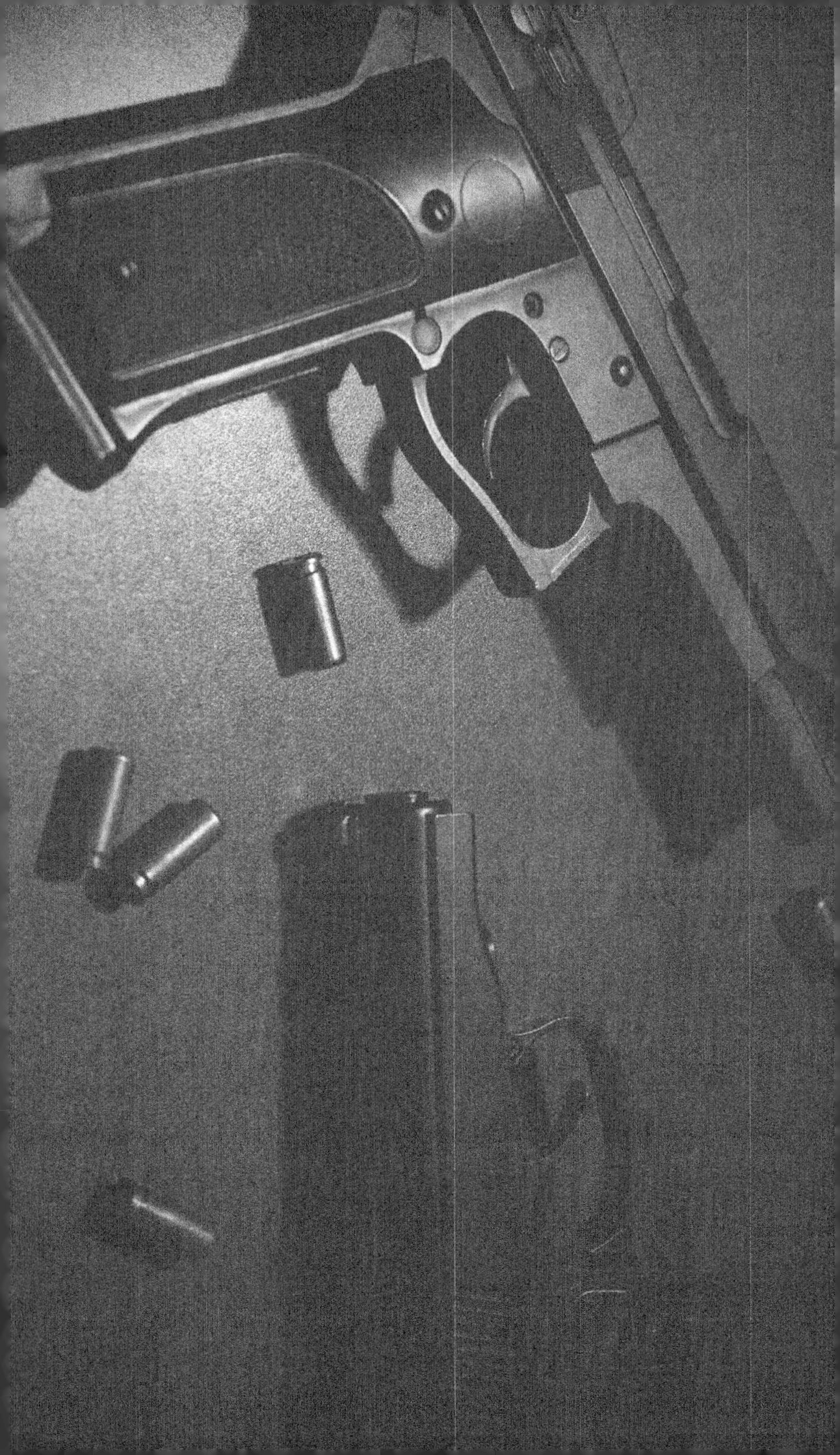

# Chapter Nineteen

## Viktor

For the first time in a while, I sleep through the night. No distractions, no stress. Just me and Amaia.

I'm surprised that she trusted me enough to tie her down, not once using her safe word. She's like everything I've ever dreamed of. The perfect woman to me. I pull her closer against me, not yet wanting to leave the bed. But I know I need to. My chef will be here soon for breakfast, and before that I need to make a call. Make sure Dmitri's body has been dumped. Hopefully, it will bring Ivan out of hiding.

I pull my arm out gently from under her, covering her back up with the sheets, no matter how much I'd rather stare at her. I'm sure she'd appreciate being covered up. Picking up my pants, I quickly pull them on and sneak out of the bedroom. I pull up my contacts and step into my office. I sit on my large wingback leather chair and lean back.

"Did you get rid of it?" I ask by way of greeting. Konstantin is used to me being blunt in the most important matters.

His gruff voice answers immediately, "We did last night, boss."

"Perfect. We will have a meeting later this evening. We need to talk backup plans for Ivan. None of them will include using Amaia as bait." I have to mention her, as everyone now knows she is Ivan's daughter, but she is also off-limits.

"We'll keep an eye on her too," he promises.

I hang up, not needing anything else. I consider giving Konstantin a raise for dealing with me. I'll see how things work out after The Koskovich's are dealt with. A deep sigh leaves my chest, at least that's one thing out the way. I leave my office and walk downstairs.

My chef, Joan, smiles as she enters the front door, her greying hair in a tight bun. The wrinkles crinkle in the corner of her eyes reminding me of my mother. They would be the same age right now if she were still alive . "Good morning, Mister Petrov. I'm sorry I am late. I'll get your breakfast prepared right now." She hangs up her coat and rushes through the foyer and dining room and into the kitchen, putting on the clean white apron over her beige pants and white shirt. She gathers some ingredients to prepare breakfast. .

I lean against the countertop and quickly gaze out the window. "Please, I've told you many times, just call me Viktor. Also, I have a special guest with me this morning. Can you make sure to make an extra dish for her, please?" I turn back to her with a smile, I always respect my staff. I've known Joan for a long time, and I don't like to see her as an employee. She's a friend. I'd be lost without her.

"Of course, Mister...Viktor." She nods, a small smile twitching in the corner of her mouth. I never bring women home and keep them in my room all night.

I'm pulled from my thoughts when small footsteps come from the stairs. Amaia appears, still wearing my shirt. She freezes and pulls down at the hem as if it could cover anything else. Even though it already reaches her knees.

"Actually, I have to go. I need to train," she stammers, mentioning her ballet.

My brows furrow. She has a sweet, innocent voice that would sound convincing, but she doesn't have to go. Training this hard after a show isn't mandatory. I researched ballet stuff to try and get the hang of it for when I finally got her to myself.

She tucks her hair behind her ears and gives me a small smile before running back up the stairs. I apologize to Joan and follow Amaia. She is using training as an excuse to skip a meal.

I push the door open as she's looking for other clothes to wear, but she stops when she notices me.

"You don't need to train. After last night, you should relax. Let me treat you today."

She shakes her head. "I can't. I'm fulfilling my dreams, and no man can get in my way. I promised myself years ago. If I call in sick, I can't go to the celebration this evening either."

I raise a brow; I must be slacking. There had not been any word about a party from my team. There was nothing on Amaia's phone or laptop with dates marked. I narrow my gaze.

Stepping towards her until she's backed up against my dresser, I ask, "What celebration?"

But she bites her lip and shakes her head. "Just something we do after a week of shows. It's no big deal. I just need to be there."

"Then I'll go too. One of my drivers will take you home." I step away from her, opening up a drawer to pass her some boxers of mine so she is at least covered up underneath as I send her home. She opens her mouth to protest, but I shut her up with a kiss instead, leaving the room straight after.

"You can't come to this," she calls out, but I don't care.

I'll be there. She may be saying no to me now, but I could see it in her eyes. She wants me to be there.

Instead of telling her that, I call out, "And Joan will box you up some breakfast. She will be insulted if you don't eat it." Joan won't, but using that as an excuse might make Amaia more inclined to actually eat. At least, that's my hope.

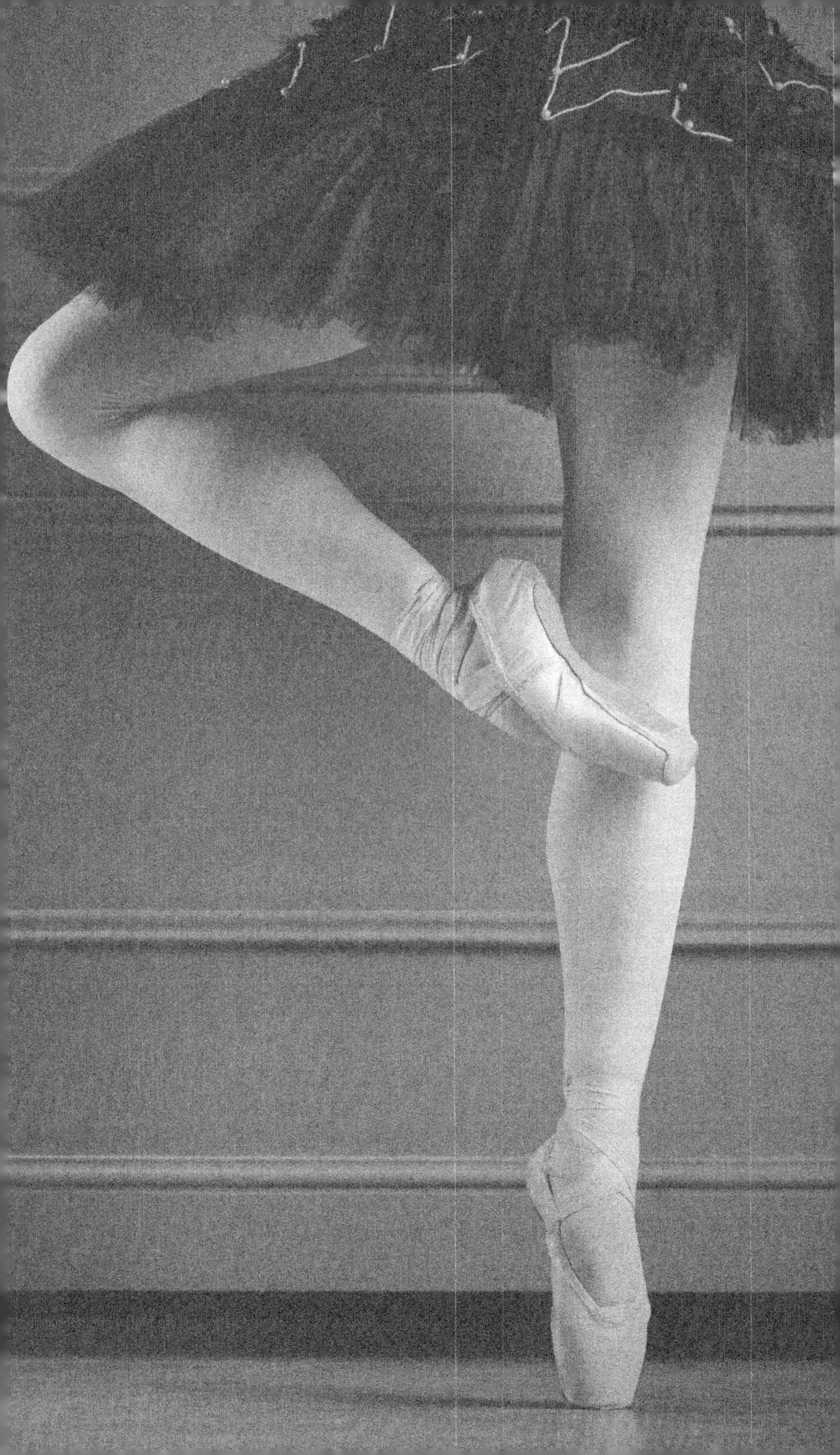

# Chapter Twenty

## Amaia

I'm honestly not surprised that Viktor said he would see me here. After his driver dropped me off, I ate some of what Joan made for breakfast. It was good, but I couldn't eat too much. Just a few bites. Training wouldn't have been easy on a bloated stomach.

I'm surprised I was able to stretch after last night. I'm glad my bite mark has gone down, too. The girls still make comments about it, and Damien can barely look at me. I think he is annoyed with me, but he was my closest friend in the studio. So I caught up with him after training, and we talked. He said I had become distant since meeting Viktor, and the girls are only talking about me because they feel that they are picking up on the movements that I'm failing on.

So, I took my time to think while getting ready for the

celebration tonight. How I am going to get Viktor to back off, give me more time to train. Let me fulfill my dreams. I guess I didn't even realize that's what I had been doing.

I decided that tonight I'd wear burgundy instead of my usual black for parties. A beautiful backless silk dress that stopped mid-thigh. I wear my hair in loose waves that end at my waist, just a hint of makeup making my face glow. I finish my look with my diamond tennis bracelet my dad sent me for my eighteenth birthday. I had only worn it once before, out of spite.

I push my way through the doors of the rented hall, musical instruments harmonize the room with undertones of glasses clinking. A couple of people turn to me. Damien is one of them, calling me over to large french windows with thick deep purple drapes. I walk over the glossy hardwood floors, my heels tap along with each step. He hands me a glass of champagne from the waiter with a tray full of them.

"Thank you," I tell him, taking a sip. He leans forward, his strong cologne hits me and I try my hardest not to move away. But looks over my head instead, and his jaw clenches.

"Amaia," a deep voice says from behind me.

Shivers run over my body, and I turn to face Viktor. I bite my lip, looking him up and down. No matter how discrete I try to be, he smirks and leans in, kissing me.

I stay still, in shock, and when he pulls away, he grins. My lipstick is smeared across his lips.

"I don't remember inviting you," I blurt, panicking when all eyes are on us. Immediately, I wish I could retract what I said.

But he merely brushes hair out of my face and says, "You didn't have to, little doll. I'll always be there for you."

My heart does a little flip, and I try to squash it down. But based on the smirk on Viktor's face, I wasn't able to hide my reaction. Instead, I take another sip of my champagne.

I feel other eyes on me as Viktor wraps his arm around my waist. I nervously chew my lip; this is new to me. I've never been very public with affection, maybe at most holding hands. My body has never been pressed up against a man while he kisses my cheek.

It's bad enough that Viktor marked me before with his bite. His hand sensually drifts down to my hip and draws small circles on the fabric of my dress, as though he is caressing my body subconsciously.

Looking up at him, I smile. "Can we speak in private, please?" I ask.

He needs to leave. Important people are here. Ones that control my future, if they see me act inappropriately, I might not be considered for Prima.

He guides me to a nearby hallway. We can still hear the chatter through the doors, but for now we have privacy. I open my mouth to speak, but Viktor takes advantage of my silence and kisses me.

His hand fist my hair, tilting my head back. I'm momentarily shocked when he pulls away, and my eyes flutter open. He casually takes a sip of his champagne and presses his thumb on my lower lip. My mouth parts for him, and he leans in, his own lips hovering above mine.

He spits the champagne in my mouth. "Swallow what I give you, Amaia."

With my eyes on his, I obey.

"Can you stay quiet, little doll?" he asks with a raised eyebrow.

"What?" I ask, in a daze.

His hand rests against the front of my dress, slowly gliding down until he reaches the hem. Pressing his body closer to mine, his fingers move between my thighs and press against my silk-covered clit.

I suck in a sharp breath. His rough fingers rip my panties to the side, thrusting his thick fingers inside me. I grip his shoulders, trying to hold in a moan.

"You're wet. You liked it," he chuckles.

I tremble beneath his touch. "No," I lie.

"Tsk, tsk, your body says otherwise." He thrusts more fingers inside and moves slowly, curling his fingers to press against my g-spot.

My hips move to match his rhythm, chasing the orgasm I can already feel building. My eyes flutter closed, and my head leans back against the wall. Then he pulls his fingers out, and I whimper at the loss.

"Bad girls don't get to come. Stand by me all night, do everything I say, and I'll reward you later." He lifts his fingers to my mouth. "Now suck them clean." His fingers brush against my lower lip.

I do as he says and open my mouth to suck my arousal

off of him.

"That's my good girl," he praises. Warmth spreads throughout my body. Never in my life has anyone's words affected my body like this.

"Let's go back to the party," Viktor says, guiding me back in.

I never got to ask him to leave, but I stay by his side for the rest of the night instead. We even dance. I ignore everyone's gaze on us.

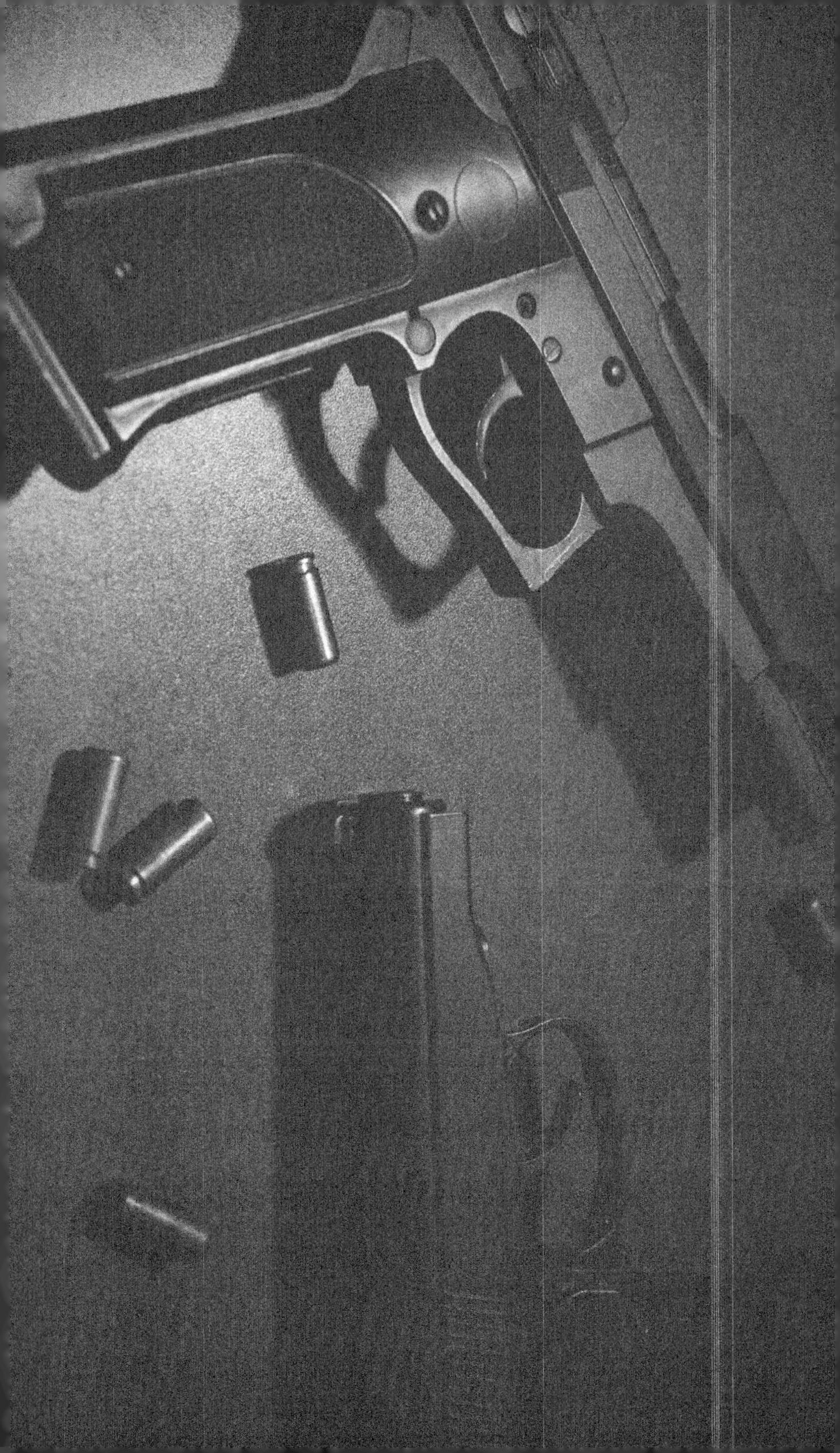

# Chapter Twenty-One

# Viktor

"Strip," I demand, and Amaia's pretty red mouth drops open.

She looks absolutely ravishing tonight, and I've been desperate to get her back home all evening. But I needed people to see us, to know she is unavailable. She belongs to *me*.

We're back in my playroom and I dim the lights, knowing she feels more comfortable this way; it's almost romantic. Internally, I shake my head. Nope. Not going there.

Amaia obeys and pushes the straps of her dress over her shoulders, letting the soft silk drop down her perfect body. She hooks her fingers into her panties and removes them easily.

"Lay back and spread your legs for me."

She takes a few steps backwards until her knees hit the mattress and she falls back, then she starts to move further onto the bed, but stops. Her heels are still on.

She reaches down towards the straps, but I hold up my hand. "Leave them on."

Amaia nods and stays quiet, continuing to shimmy to the pillows. She spreads her legs, offering me her pussy like a sweet dessert that I will all too soon devour. A low growl leaves my throat.

Her glistening arousal calls to me, to fuck her until my bed breaks.

I stalk toward her, pulling out a spreader bar that is hidden in plain sight on the bedpost. I strap her ankles to it, then move to her wrists. I restrain her there against the headboard again. She tries to move but can't, her brief struggle sending a jolt to my hardness. I remove my tie and thread it through my fingers.

"Don't blindfold me. I want to see you." She bites down on her lip, waiting for my response.

I raise my eyebrow. This usually goes my own way. But I do as she asks and hang my tie over a chair, along with the rest of my clothes as I peel them off. Her eyes trace deliciously along my body, her gaze finally coming to rest on my cock.

I grab the base and move my hand up over myself, groaning and imagining it's her touching me.

My finger runs over the tip of my hardness, collecting the bead of precum. Then I wipe it along her lower lip. Her tongue flicks out, tasting me.

"I'm going to fuck your face," I tell her, warning her of what's to come.

"But you've tied me down?" she retorts.

I just smirk and straddle her chest, guiding my cock to her mouth. She wets her lips and opens for me. With one hand leaning on the wall and the other keeping her head in a comfortable position, I thrust deep into her throat.

She moans, and the vibrations on her lips drive me forward, wanting more. I thrust harder, feeling the back of her throat. Her eyes water and tears fall, staining her cheeks with the remaining makeup she was wearing.

"I love seeing you cry like this, my cock in your mouth. Making choking noises as I hit the back of your throat. You feel fucking amazing."

My balls tighten. Pulling her head closer, I'm pretty sure

she can't breathe at this point. But now I'm coming hard down her throat, and I won't pull out until every last drop is swallowed. That was way too quick for my liking.

She takes it all greedily, and I slip out, my cock softening.

"Are you okay?" I ask as she takes deep breaths. I use my thumb to wipe away the tears that had fallen, raising my eyebrow when she doesn't answer.

But she nods; I've taken her breath away.

"You did so well," I praise her. She offers me a little smile, the same one she does every time I praise her. I'm not sure if she notices it or not, but I love it. "You're my good fucking girl, understand?"

"Yes, sir," she says breathlessly.

She pulls against her restraints, and I shake my head with a tsk. "I'm not done with you yet." I grin and grab a collar and extra restraints.

Her eyes widen. I can't tell if it's from panic or curiosity. Either way, she has her words.

Fastening the collar I bought just for her around her neck, I make sure it's not too tight and then attach two individual straps to the hoop around her neck. I move my hand over her body until I reach the bar between her legs, and I pull it up until her knees hit her shoulders. I use the straps and strap her ankles to them to hold her in place. She can't move at all. Knees to chest, completely spread out.

"Tell me your words," I say gruffly. I can't start unless I know. "I need your stop and slow down safe words."

"Red to stop," she tells me, biting her lip.

"And?" I continue to question. The rest of tonight will be all about her. I need to make sure she enjoys every second, even if she needs me to back off.

"Yellow to slow down?" she suggests.

I climb between her legs, staring down at the most perfect pussy I have ever seen. "I wish you could see yourself right now, all spread out for me. I'm getting hard again already." I press my growing cock against her thigh so she can feel the truth in my words.

"Then fuck me," she begs, writhing beneath her bonds.

I chuckle and spank her clit, "I'll fuck you when I'm finished eating you." She moans, and I spank her again. "I love how sensitive you get."

Leaning down, I flick my tongue on her clit. Hearing her calling my name again, I suck on it and thrust a finger inside her.

I groan. "You're fucking soaking. Is that what my cock in your mouth does to you?"

I take my fingers out and fuck her with my tongue instead. My nose is pressing against her sensitive bundle of nerves. She starts chanting my name like a mantra until she finally cries out and comes all over my face.

She whimpers when I pull away and lean back up. I rub my cock along her slit twice, coating the tip in her orgasm, then I force myself in. The way she's restrained and kept in this position is making it easier to go deeper and fuck, it's tighter.

I slowly slide out, watching where we are joined and thrusting back in. Harder this time. I continue to fuck her, the headboard slamming against the wall to the rhythm of my thrusts.

An orchestra of our moans fill the room, and fuck, I don't want to cum yet, but I'm so close. I press her clit with my thumb and circle. Her eyes roll to the back of her head, and her pussy strangles my cock as another orgasm crashes through her and I soon join her, roaring with my own release.

We don't say or do anything. Our heavy breathing is the only sound in the room. I hold myself up on my forearm to stop myself from collapsing on her.

My whole body is vibrating. Eventually, I gather the energy to move when Amaia looks completely crushed under me. But her face is glowing, and she's smiling, so I know she's not hurt. A warmth runs through my chest beneath the thumping of my own heart.

I immediately pull out, admiring her cum all over my dick and balls. Instead of overthinking my feelings. Reaching over, I unclip the restraints holding Amaia's knees to her chest, and help lower her legs. I massage every part of her that I touch. Hopefully, she doesn't have cramps. I flick the ring of the collar, enjoying the way it looks on her, knowing I want this permanent.

We match. Her mind is in chaos. Letting me control her in this way calms her. My eyes meet hers, and I can't help but notice the scorching desire still there. "You're mine," I growl. She nods, and I kiss her on the lips. "I'm going to run us a bath."

Then I leave her on the bed.

I stare down in my large bathtub as water fills it. It was pride. That's what I'd felt before. Nothing else. I can't overthink this.

I search the bathroom to find something for her, then pour in some bubble bath to help Amaia relax.

While the bath is still filling, I go back to the bed and undo the rest of the restraints and lift her in my arms to carry her into the bathroom.

Her eyes squint as we enter, the bright lights stunning her for a brief moment. I place her on the counter and dim these lights too. Reaching out my hand, I wait for her to take it. Softly, I guide her to the tub with me, and she leans against me as we lay back, humming as we sink in further.

"This is nice," she murmurs, her voice laced with content.

I kiss her shoulder and hum into her skin. My hands knead the muscles on her upper back, knowing she will need it. Then I turn her in the water so I can do her legs, taking extra care so she won't be sore tomorrow.

She leans back and closes her eyes, I've never seen her so relaxed around me. I would usually just shower with my girls, take care of them so they don't have a sub drop. But Amaia, she's different. I want this moment to be burned into my memory forever. Just her, so open around me. It's completely different from when we first met.

The more I watch her, the more I realize that the feeling from long ago was not pride, no matter how much I tell myself that it is. It was more, so much more. I want to keep her.

The only question is, would she want me back? That's what's stopping me from asking for more. She is too good for me.

But I'm also a selfish man.

So maybe I'll keep her like this until she falls for me. No turning back.

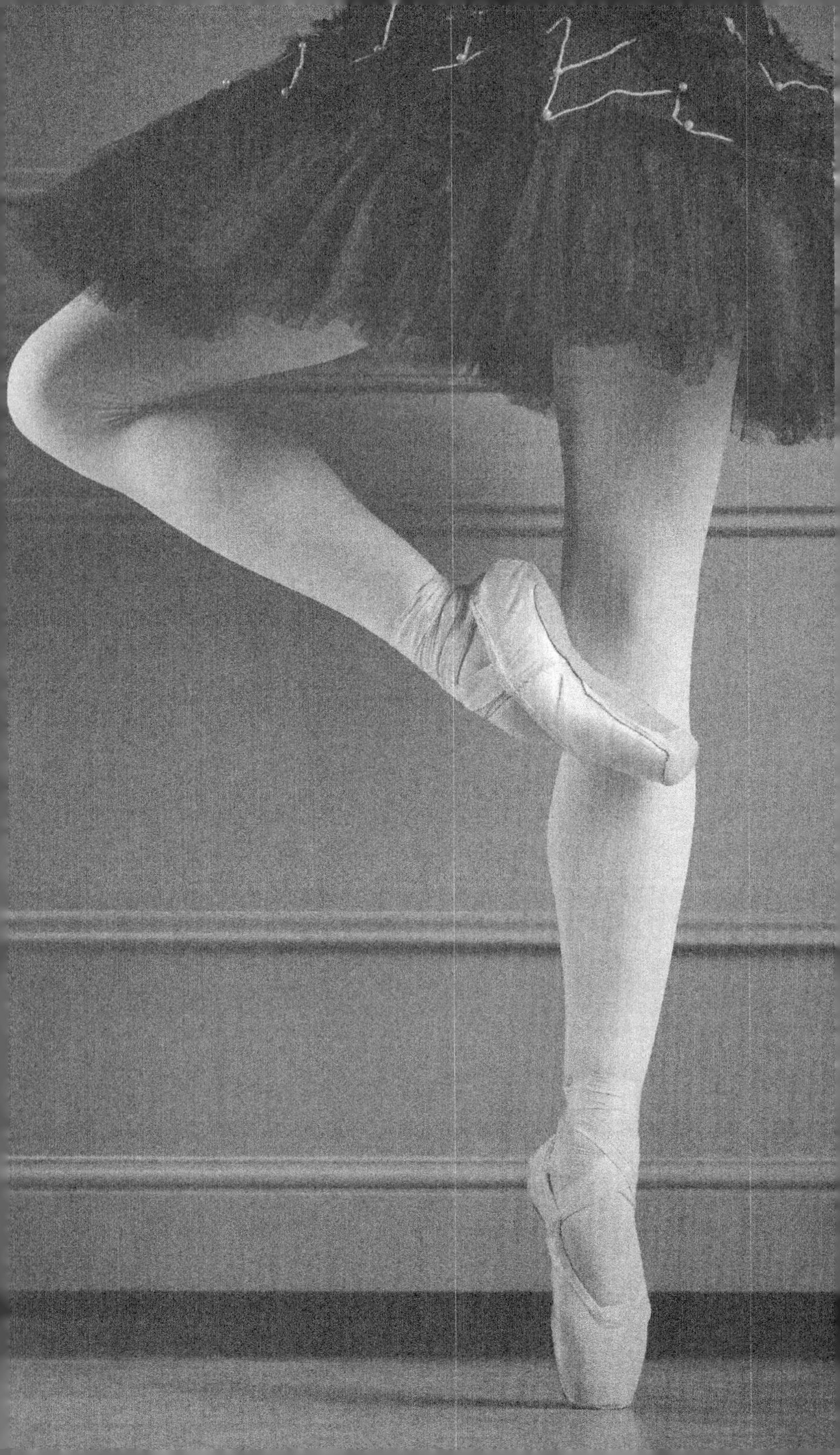

# Chapter Twenty-Two

# Amaia

After our bath, Viktor went quiet. I'm not sure if I did something wrong. I try not to let it get to me, but the thought stays with me, clawing at my mind. Even while he runs his fingers through my hair, he is deep in thought. I wish I could read his mind for just one day.

We now lay in bed, watching a cheesy movie while he feeds me strawberries. Another hot chocolate each. He says I need it, although I hate thinking about the calories.

But I also made an appointment with a specialist doctor a few weeks ago, and we've been talking once a week about my thoughts on food. The doctor said it sounds like body dysmorphia. I see a distorted image of myself when I look in the mirror.

We have been working together to help me see a healthier version of myself. So I drank those calories.

When Viktor and I are together, he makes me feel calm and level-headed. I don't have the urge to control everything in my life as much. For just a moment, I let it all go and let him take charge. Dancing is a large part of my life and needs control. But when I'm done training I go to him.

Eventually, I drift off in his arms, a soft smile on my face. Just as I'm about to sleep, his lips press against my hair, and it makes me feel precious.

"Sleep well, beautiful," he whispers.

A low ringtone pulls me from my light sleep. It's my phone. Viktor grumbles as I get up and stumble to my bag, pulling it out. An unknown number shines on the screen. I press the green button and answer.

"Miss Frost?" a grumbly voice comes from the other end.

"Yes?" I answer hesitantly, glancing at the time. 5 a.m. It

can't be the ballet association this early.

"This is the L.A.P.D. Could you come to the station? We need to speak with you. It's an urgent matter." He sighs deeply.

"What's wrong? Has something happened?" As soon as the words leave my lips, Viktor is up and pulling on clothes. Without listening to what else he has to say. I rush out, "I'll be there soon, officer."

Viktor passes me my dress and a jacket of his to cover the rest of me. We both are silent as we get in his car. His cool and calm demeanor freaks me out. How can someone be so calm after getting a call to come into the police station? This is something serious, and I can't stop my knee from bouncing, even as we pull into the parking lot.

I rush through the doors, straight past the empty chairs of the waiting area, with Viktor following close behind. I stare at the tired receptionist sitting behind the desk. The stench of old coffee wafts from the cup beside her. "I'm Amaia Frost. Someone called me to come in?"

Viktor wraps his arm around my waist, gripping me tightly.

The jangling of keys pulls my attention to a tall police

officer as he comes through a door, gesturing for me approach, and we both move. The officer looks at Viktor. "Sir, I need you to stay out here. This won't be long."

I press my hand on Viktor's chest, finding his heart is beating fast beneath my palm. "It's okay, just wait here." I give him a small smile, a lie, because there is a bad feeling settling in my stomach.

With every step that officer takes me to a small room, I want to turn back and have Viktor hold my hand. But I'm a big girl. I can do this alone.

I'm guided to a small room with a desk and two seats, the officer sits on a chair opposite the small plastic chair that he gestures for me to sit, a sympathetic look passes over his face and he shuffles the paper. "Your brother is Dmitri Koskovich, correct?" he asks.

My brows dip, and I nod slowly. "Yes, he is."

My hands start trembling; I just know what this news is. He gets in trouble with the men he works for. He hadn't been answering his phone, and I haven't seen him since the night of my show weeks ago. Nothing. I kept telling myself he is involved in drugs and will turn up soon... but it's too late.

"I'm sorry, Miss Frost. We found your brother's body late yesterday."

Any other words he says are drowned out by the deafening roar of disbelief spiralling through my head. All those times that I could have called and left a voicemail instead of hanging up in frustration.

I could have checked up on him, but I was busy. Being selfish and putting myself first. My career.

"Can I see him?" I whisper, my heart like a lead weight in my chest.

Another person is abandoning me. My dad left when I was a kid, my mom is with her new boyfriend traveling the world and rarely answers her phone. My brother was all I had left.

The officer scratches the back of his head and a solemn look flashes across his face.

"I'm not sure that's not a good idea. He had to be identified using dental records." He huffs out a breath, and an uncomfortable silence descends on us.

He was unrecognizable.

Images of his face cross my mind, and I try to shake them away. He must have been scared. What kind of monsters could do something like this?

I'm still sat on that uncomfortable plastic chair in the

interview room for thirty minutes as they speak to me, one- or two-word answers coming from me for everything they ask. I'm not sure there is anything I can do. "Just find who did this."

Eventually, they let me go.

He was murdered. They don't know who did it, and it's likely they never will. He was involved in gangs, and their theory is most likely another dealer that he screwed over.

The click of my heels is the only sound I register as I walk through the corridor back out into the waiting room.

Viktor sits on the chairs fingers tapping on his knees, when he notices me he rushes over, concern written on his face. He pulls me close. "What happened? Are you okay?"

I don't hold him back, instead only lean into his chest and tell him the truth.

"Someone murdered my brother."

He stays silent for a moment, then holds me tighter. I pull myself from his embrace. "I need to go home." I turn and leave, hiding the tears that won't stop falling, and his footsteps follow. He takes me home, no questions.

We don't talk, we don't touch.

We just lay in my bed while I try not to imagine all the ways Dmitri died and why they couldn't show me his face.

I don't go back to sleep.

The sun rises hours later, and Viktor sits up. "I need to go to a quick meeting, then I'll take some time off to stay with you."

I nod and turn away.

His footsteps disappear, and the door closes downstairs. I try to go back to sleep, but it becomes impossible. I keep asking myself if there is anything I could have done, anything to stop it. Maybe if I never asked him to come to my shows or begged more often to quit the gangs.

When the sun has fully risen, I give up and throw on some sweatpants and a t-shirt. Again, I avoid the mirror, knowing there will be dark circles under my puffy eyes.

A loud knock makes me jump, and I peek out the bedroom window and see it's Damien. I'm not sure if I want to see anyone today, but the knocking comes more insistent. "I'm coming!" I call out.

I rip open the door and Damien pushes through, shoves me out the way, and locks the door. I step away from him, eyeing him warily.

"What's going on?" My heart speeds up, and I take another step back, my eyes flicking between him and the lock on the door. He lunges toward me and grabs my wrist.

"What are you doing? You're hurting me."

I try to yank my arm back, but he's stronger than me.

His words are insistent: "You're in danger. Pack a bag. I can get us somewhere safe."

I attempt to pull back again, and he lets me go. Viktor will hurt him if he finds out Damien came here and grabbed me.

"I'm fine," I say stiffly. "I'm protected." At least, I hope so. Viktor had been keeping me guarded, following me. Why would everything change now?

Damien's eyes dart around, and he lowers his voice, stepping closer. "Your boyfriend is a murderer. Come with me; I know someone who can help you get away. Keep you safe."

I cut him a sharp look. "Viktor is not my boyfriend." I'm ignoring the murder comment.

I sidestep Damien and walk away, trying not to make it obvious I'm walking a little faster so I can reach the back door. I don't get far before a rag covers my mouth and nose, and I instinctively kick and scratch in an attempt to break free. Glass smashes as the heel of my foot connects with something.

I'm lifted just as everything goes black.

Blinking my eyes open, I lift my hand to cover my face, shielding my vision from the blinding light above me. I try to turn, but a handcuff is wrapped around my left wrist, trapping me to a bed. I pull against it, hoping it's weak and will break, but it's not. There's a nightstand next to me with a clock on it, I've been unconscious for a few hours.

"Morning, Princess," an old but familiar voice says from the doorway of the room. My breath catches at the sight of him, his dark brown hair now peppered with whites. The high cheekbones is the only thing I had inherited and his burning gaze goes straight through me. Dmitri looks just like him.

"Dad?" I gasp, and he smiles, but all I can think is why?

Why couldn't he come and visit?

Why did he just leave?

Why couldn't he be a dad to me as well as Dmitri?

Staring him in the eyes, I blurt, "Mom said it's safer without you around. I'm pretty sure she hates you now." Maybe that's why she never sticks around; I remind her of him.

He sighs, "I'm sorry it's been so long. I've been building our family business. We have enemies, and I had to make it safe. Dmitri and I were clearing space here. That Petrov family tried taking us out years ago. But it didn't work, and now we are coming back stronger. That was until the Petrov killed Dmitri." He shakes his head and pinches his nose. "And I'm sorry about the kidnapping. I had to get you away without a fight."

My heart sinks when my dad pulls out a folder and sits on the side of the mattress.

"This is why I had guards growing up?" I ask, trying to hide the trembling in my voice.

"Yes, everyone was disappointed that you asked your brother to call off the bodyguards once you turned fifteen, but we know how things were. A teenage girl with two men following her." My father shakes his head with a rueful grin. "They were still there, but they must have been slacking as you grew older. It's like they trusted you to do the right thing."

"I never knew who he was—" I try to explain, hoping he would believe my lie.

My father waves his hand away and picks up the folder. He pulls out some photos of Viktor dealing drugs, holding a gun to someone's head, and him standing over a dead body. I couldn't look after that even though there were plenty more pictures. Just because Viktor does these things, it doesn't mean I want to be involved and especially not see him doing it. I wanted to stay oblivious, like I had been this whole time.

"Please leave me alone," I say quietly, but my father hears me.

"I'll send food up. When you feel like you are ready to make a deal, let your friend know. I'm sure you understand that I need to keep you locked in here. Since you have been involved with the enemy." He pats my leg and stands.

I can't say anything, so I look away. My life has been tipped upside down since I met Viktor.

I even got Damien wrong. Is every man in my life a liar?

I'm not sure how long it's been, but the sun is going down. I must have been lying here for hours lost in my thoughts. I sit up when I hear the slide of a lock on the door. Damien walks in holding a tray with a small smile that I don't return.

"I'm not hungry," I tell him.

He places it on the vanity table and sits on the bed with me. "I imagine this isn't how you thought your day would go, but we can't shield you anymore. Everything will be okay here. You have me, and your dad won't leave you behind."

I turn away and face the window again. Until a hand lands on my upper thigh. I try to move away, but I'm crushed up against the headboard. He moves closer, his grip growing tighter.

"Why not me? I've been here all along. We could have been perfect together." His hand moves further up.

"I've only ever seen you as a friend." I keep my voice soft, but he grabs my other leg and pulls me to face him. I knock him away with my one free hand.

A sick feeling settles in my stomach at the look in his eye. It's not one I've seen on him before. His eyes are dark, and he licks his lips. Grabbing both my legs, he pulls me back to him. I slap him with the one hand I have available, opening my mouth to shout, but he covers it with his hand.

"Shut the fuck up." Something in him snaps; he turns feral, and I fight against him.

His other hand pulls at my sweatpants, and when they reach my ankles, I try to kick him away, but it doesn't work.

He grabs at my panties. I attempt to scream, hot tears pouring from my eyes, but no one can hear me. I scrunch my eyes shut, trying to block out the inevitable. He's stronger than me, and I'm handcuffed. I can keep fighting, but he will continue to take what doesn't belong to him.

The moment he pulls my thighs apart, something happens outside. Gunshots.

Damien is ripped away, and I curl into myself. My heart is trying to escape my chest—it's pounding so hard. Everything is blurred as more men come in, and one approaches me.

"I've got you," Viktor's voice washes over me as he pulls my clothes back on. I'm just glad Damien didn't get any further.

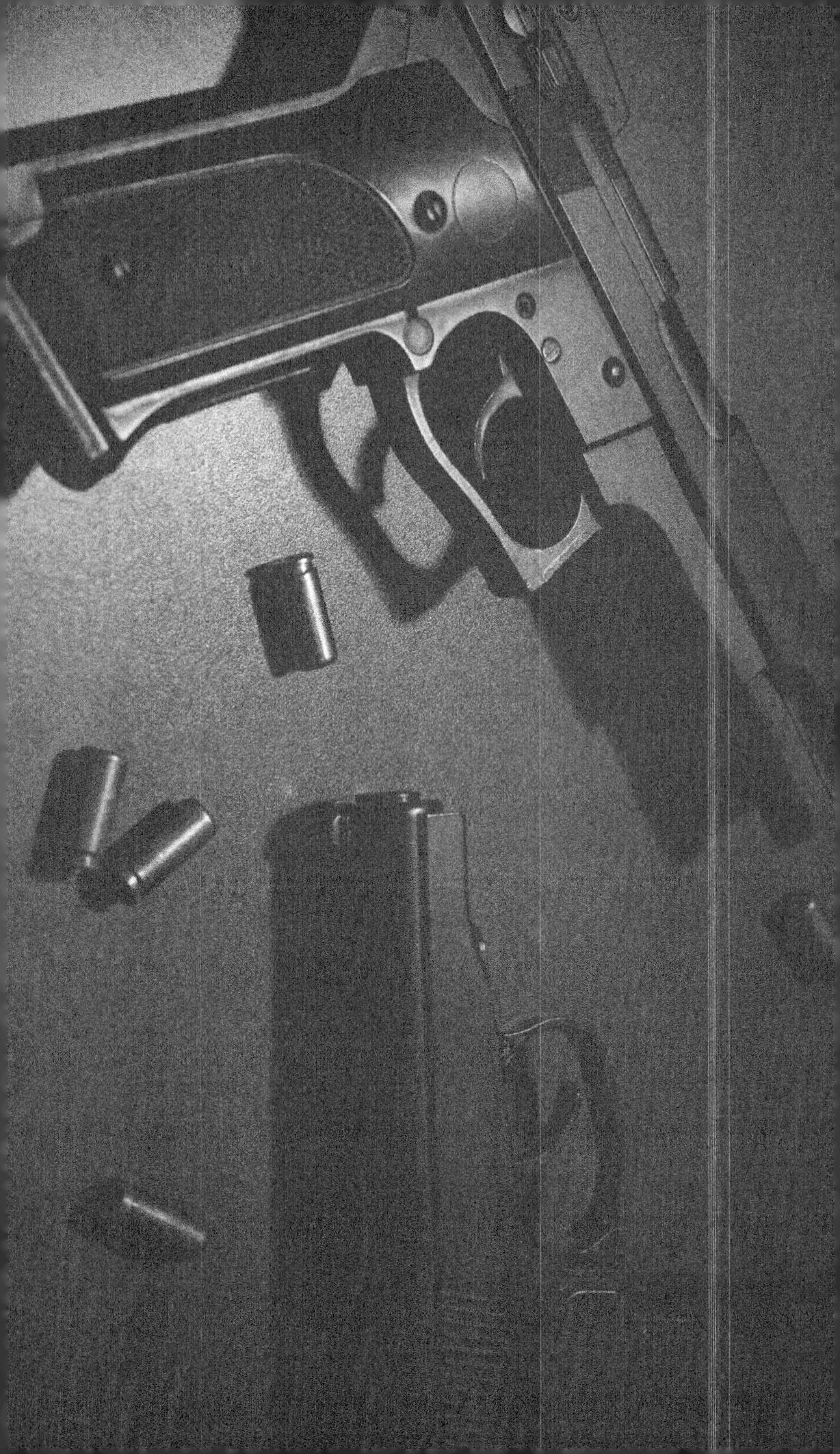

# Chapter Twenty-Three

## Viktor

<u>Three hours earlier</u>

I'm with Konstantin and my main supplier for our next delivery. We're all sitting around the large table when there's a commotion outside. The door bursts open, and I pull my gun on who it is. But my stomach drops when I see the guard I left with Amaia, blood running down the side of his head and his eyes wide and panicked.

"Where is she?" I step toward him, gun still pointed as rage builds inside me.

"They took her. That male friend of hers came. Pushed his way inside, so I stepped outside my car to make sure she was okay, but someone hit me over the head and knocked me out. When I woke up, I checked inside. There was a tipped over table and smashed photo frame. A rag was nearby."

A deadly calm washes over me as we stare at each other. I knew there was something wrong with that Damien. I should have dealt with him weeks ago. FUCK.

I bark, "Someone trace the fucker's phone, I want him alive." I don't address anyone specific; I just want it done. Now. I need her found and if anything happens to her, I will kill whoever who gets in my way.

A chorus of "Yes, boss," fills the room and everyone stands and rushes toward the door. Two minutes it takes for the hacker to be brought in. I step over his shoulder Watching the screen hoping for answers. Then I pace. I should have put a tracker on her; it would have saved time. It's something my father would do.

All eyes are on me, waiting for my next command. *Please be okay. I'm coming for you.*

"Boss," the hacker calls me over, and my head snaps toward him. "We have a location."

I start walking away, calling out, "Text it to me." There is no time to waste.

As I reach my land rover, I vow that if she is hurt in any

way, I'll tear them apart, piece by piece. Then send their limbs to others as a warning.

But first, I need a way in and out with Amaia unharmed and in my arms.

---

We burst through the doors, firing out guns through the small foyer as we rush through to the great room. My men spread out and I duck behind a small fabric chair when a bullet grazes my arm. Ivan. He smirks, and I shoot him in the kneecaps before he runs away, he drops in front of the unlit fireplace.

I turn to one of my men and nod my head in Ivan's direction. "Grab him. I want him alive."

As we shoot our way through, I notice Amaia isn't down here, so I rush up the large staircase. Over the sound of gunshots, I hear her muffled screams. I don't even think; I kick the door open and see that fucker Damien on top of her. A roar escapes my throat and I charge in toward him

I rip him back, smashing his head against the wall to knock him out. Blood drips down the side of his head, leaving a splatter of red against the soft pink walls.

"Amaia," I murmur as I approach her. Her eyes are wide, her tear-streaked face not looking at me.

Someone passes me a key from the unconscious fucker, and I set her wrist free and cover the injury from where she had been pulling against it to get away. I help pull on her clothes and hold her to my chest, then shout out to my men to grab him too. She sobs against me, desperately holding onto my shirt.

I can't stand to see her like this. I need to kill them all slowly. Or better, keep them alive so Amaia can take her revenge.

"Take them both to the warehouse in separate containers," I snap as I carry Amaia out the door.

Getting in the car, I lay her across my lap in the backseat. Konstantin comes out not long after us and drives us back without a word. The others have another car, so I can concentrate on getting her safe at mine. I've probably just started a war, but she is worth it.

When we arrive at my house, I carry her to my bedroom. She doesn't say anything, she doesn't look at me. I'm not even sure if she can hear me while she's in shock. I tenderly lay her on my bed and cover her up, then call the doctor

I have on my payroll. She eventually falls asleep while we wait them to show up.

She still hasn't spoken to me or anyone since I found her. But I stay to watch over her, making sure she's safe. I brush a strand of hair from her face, giving her a soft kiss on her forehead when she cries out in her sleep. Then I move back and sit in the chair. Eventually, my eyes feel heavy, and I can't keep them open anymore.

The click of a gun pulls me from my sleep. Automatically, I reach for mine, finding it isn't on my nightstand. My head swings up, and my eyes meet hers. She's holding my own gun to me.

"You killed him. You killed Dmitri," she seethes. I clench my jaw; I tried to keep it a secret.

"You want to shoot me?" I ask.

She doesn't respond but instead takes another step back. I stand, knowing that I am scaring her when she starts shaking and uses both hands to hold up my gun. I can't bring myself to move forward and scare her again.

"Do it," I say. "If that's what you want. Do it, pull the trigger."

Her grip tightens, and tears gather on her lower lashes. She tries to blink them away. There is a strange twinge in my heart; I've had it since I found out she had been taken.

Like she would be gone forever.

"Was I just a game to you?" she whispers, but I shake my head.

"No, I didn't know who you were until after we met." It's not a lie.

"Do you even care that you killed a man?" The gun shakes in her hands, and her voice trembles. I don't move. I know the question is important to her, as it's her brother we're speaking of. But I also can't lie to her, even if she will hate me for a while.

"No, I don't. Your family killed my mother. After a war, where many others died, we made a treaty. Someone who worked with us had to marry a member of your family. For almost ten years, everything was fine. They broke it. I wouldn't take it back even if I could. He deserved it and knew it would happen. He dug his own grave."

The tears roll down her cheeks, and I long to wipe them away, knowing I'm the cause of them. I wish she could understand how my life works.

She moves back again. I keep talking. "But you, Amaia, you're the only Koskovich I would never hurt. You're the only one I would lay down my life for, because for some fucked-up reason, I found myself falling for you," I confess, my heart thumping in my ears to fill the silence between us. I want her to say something and tell me she feels the same. Or at least that she doesn't hate me.

She finally shakes her head. "You already hurt me. You made me open up to you, trust you. I let you inside my body," she cries while waving the gun around.

I need to stand firm before she hurts herself by accident. "Shoot me or give me the gun."

Her shoulders drop at the command in my voice, and she collapses to the floor in a heap, the thud of the gun instantly putting me into action. I kick the gun away and kneel in front of her, wrapping my arms around her small body, but she thrashes against me. Screaming at me not to touch her.

I know I should let go, but I can't. She's breaking, and I caused this. My eyes burn as my own emotions fight to break free. I haven't cried since my mother died. Now I'm losing another woman important to me. I don't know who I hate more right now. Me or Ivan Koskovich.

I kiss her temple. "At least let me make sure you haven't been promised to marry someone else."

She freezes in my arms. "What?"

I sigh, knowing that I'm going to hurt her more with the reality of being in the Mafia. Even if she didn't grow up with them, she is Ivan's only daughter. She won't be off-limits. Especially now that she will gain everything when Ivan is dead. They need a successor.

"Your family wants power. For that, they need connections. He could sign you away just to get a good deal. Arranged marriages happen all the time in my world. It's a business transaction." I need her to know exactly what could happen if she leaves without knowing. When she's silent, I stroke her hair from her wet cheeks.

"I'll never be safe from any of you, will I?" she mumbles, and I'm pretty sure she didn't mean to say it out loud.

I deflate. I wanted her to feel safe with me, but I'm still that fuck-up.

"You will never be off limits, not until you marry."

She sobs and pushes me away again, and this time I let her.

"The worst part about all this is that I do love you. I want to forgive you, but I can't." She angrily wipes the tears from her cheeks with a sniff. Moving on from the crying, this I can deal with easier.

"Then marry me," I say, and she stares at me with wide eyes.

"You've lost your mind." She stands and paces the floor.

I remain on my knees. "Maybe." I shrug. But I will be able to keep her safe forever.

# VIKTOR

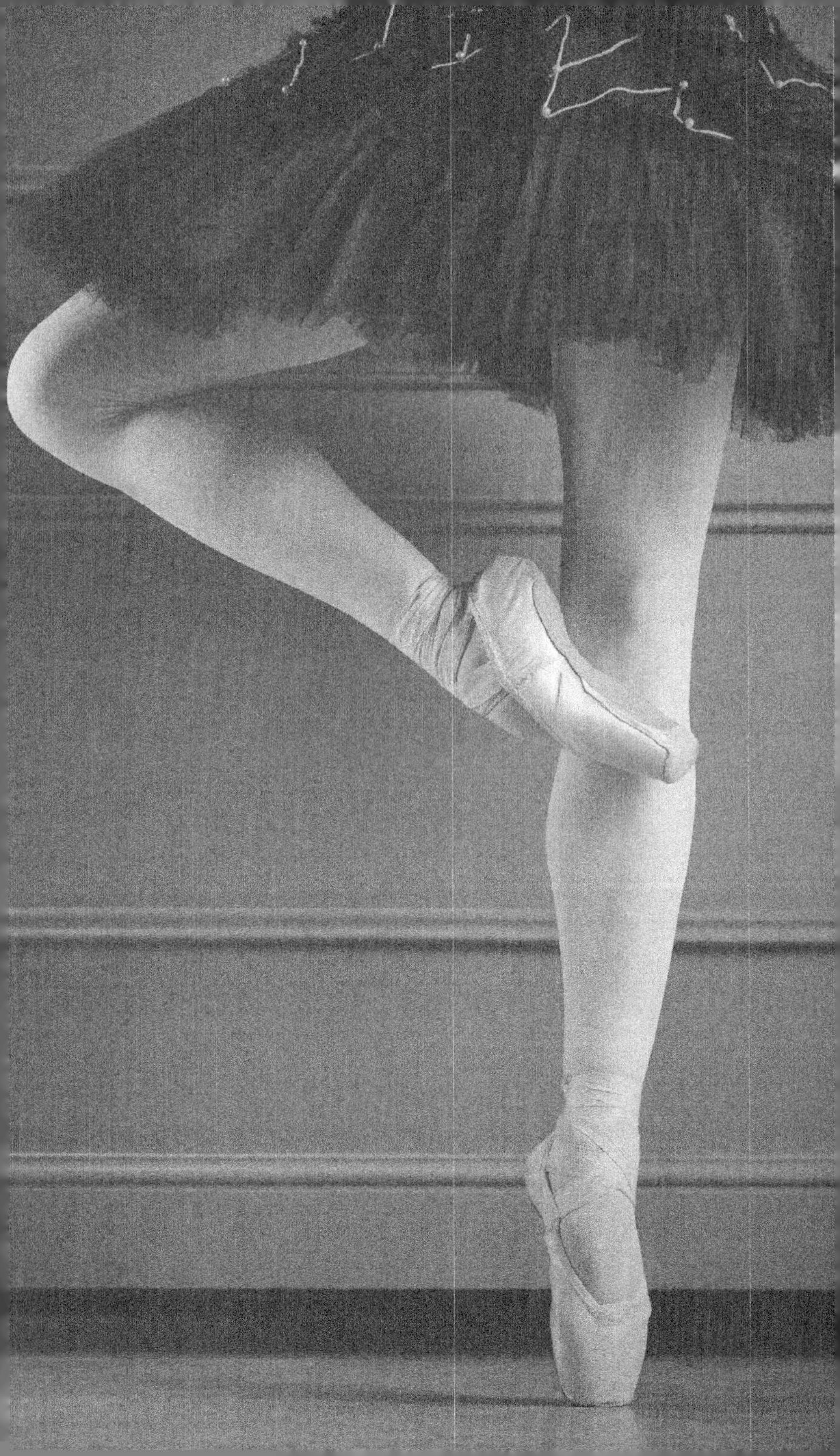

# Chapter Twenty-Four

# Amaia

He is crazy. He betrayed my trust, and now he wants me to marry him? Part of me wants to agree, as he could keep me safe from others. But the other part, the rational part, tells me to run. Leave and get as far away as possible.

If what he says is true, then I'll always be in danger. I chuckle to myself and shake my head while I'm pacing. I peer down at Viktor, who is still on his knees.

"Did you kill my dad?" I need to know; I have no doubt in my mind that Viktor would have shot him given the chance.

Viktor takes a deep breath, but never once does he takes his eyes from me. "Not yet."

I move closer to him, unsure of what I'm really doing. "And Damien?" I ask quietly, taking a step forward, even though I know I shouldn't.

He stares me in the eyes. "I'm saving him for you to punish. You choose."

I'm not sure why, but my heart speeds up. Do I want my own revenge?

Viktor grabs my hands and kisses my knuckles. "You're my everything. You decide how he is punished."

I close my eyes and imagine what I would do. Remembering his touch makes my skin crawl. Do I want to hurt him? Am I even capable?

"Do you really love me?" I ask, holding my breath.

"With everything that I am."

I'm fucked up. I think I want him, but I'm not sure if I can ever forgive him. There's a war inside my mind, and I need to pick a side. Married to a man I love, who betrayed my trust but can protect me. Or possibly being married off to some stranger by my dad and be used for breeding.

Only one of those things gives me a happy ending.

"Give me space. Take me home," I beg, but Viktor looks down and shakes his head.

"I can't do that. I need you here, where I know you will be safe." He reaches out, but I move back.

"Let me go home," I try again, my attempt at being firm with my demand failing under my trembling.

"No, not after they took you last time. I'm not risking it again."

He tries to hide it, but his voice cracks at the thought of me being taken. I'm not sure how to feel about anything anymore. If he hadn't been involved with the Mafia, he would be perfect. But is that what I want?

Is any life truly perfect? That's one of the questions I had been asked in therapy, and no, we can try over and over. If I turn Viktor away now, will I be happy?

He has been there for me through everything since we met, holding me up when I'm down. Treasuring me. Loving every part of me and my body. He takes care of me. My mind, body, and soul.

The need to hear him say it again overcomes me. "Do you really love me?" I whisper, fear spreading through my stomach at every decision I'm about to make.

"I love you, Amaia. I would start wars for you to keep you safe. To make sure you're loved." He takes a deep breath. "Ever since I saw you, when you slammed that door in my face, I've been obsessed with you."

I bite my lip, finally ready to make my decision. "Okay."

His eyebrows draw together. "What?"

"I'll marry you. But you have to know, my career is too important to me. I can't give it up to push out your children." My lips pinch into a thin line.

A grin spreads across his face as he stands. His large arms wrap around me.

"I wouldn't have you any other way."

It takes me a moment, but I hold him back. I can't second guess my choice. Out of the options I'm given, Viktor is the better one. I may not forgive him now, but maybe one day.

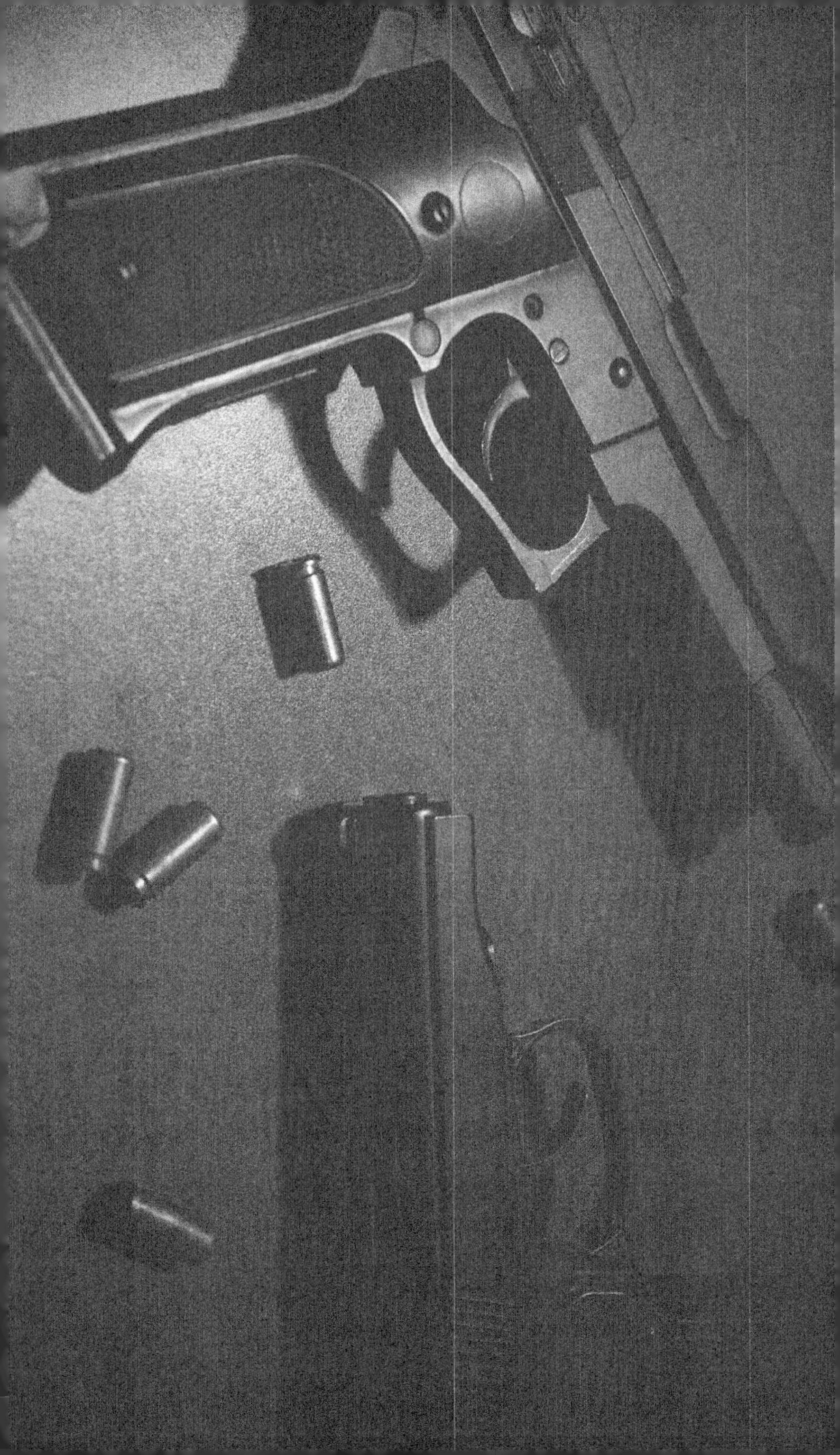

# Chapter Twenty-Five

# Viktor

Now that I finally got Amaia to marry me, I can sort out her father.

It admittedly took a while to find a large plastic tub for this. I wanted to enjoy watching him suffer. Not just because of my mother anymore; he hurt Amaia. He let another man touch her.

I step inside my warehouse, where my men have already prepared everything, and now I look at Ivan suspended on the ceiling hanging above the large plastic tub of hydrofluoric acid. I've always wanted to do this, but never before have I had the chance.

He struggles against the chains, his eyes darting from me to the scalding death awaiting him below. He knows he's fucked.

"Fuck you and your family, Petrov!" he screams.

My lip tilts up in the corner, and I shrug, lifting the little controller on the side and pressing the red button. He slowly lowers into the tub. When his toes dip in, he screams, thrashing desperately against the chains in an attempt to lift himself out.

"Where are the others?" I raise my voice so he can hear me.

I know some of his family is still out there. If they are here in L.A., then I need to find them. He shakes his head as he struggles. The skin peeling away from his feet makes me gag. It's disgusting but painful. Which he definitely deserves.

I call out again, "I don't have all day. It's Amaia's audition today. She's going to be Prima, just like she dreamed, and I won't miss watching her succeed."

He still doesn't talk. Shrugging, I press the button again until he's knee deep. I'm pretty sure the acid has eaten away at his bones by now. His screams are deafening, and I roll can't help but my eyes. He knows he can end this easily.

Konstantin and I combed through all the information we had; he hacked into all databases, and there are no more traitors here. But if they moved elsewhere, I would need to warn one of my brothers.

I glance behind me at one of my men, Igor, and he shrugs. We had spoken earlier of how much should we let him suffer. I was going to drag it out, but the screams are giving me a headache. I did hope he would beg for his life, especially with how Amaia screamed when Damien touched her.

This piece of shit let it happen. I don't know what Amaia's mother saw in him, but I'm glad they got together. Otherwise, I wouldn't have her now.

Even though we had our downs after she was taken, I fixed it. Now Konstantin watches over her, and she doesn't mind anymore. She knows it's for the best. She wouldn't let me put a tracker in her arm, though. She fought so hard against it, my little doll.

I check my watch, bored. "You have ten seconds to talk before I hold down this button and the rest of you goes in. Make the most of it."

He screeches, "Yuri is gone. Fuck y—"

I cut him off by simply pressing the red button and doing exactly as I said. His full body plunges into the acid. I take a step back when he starts thrashing. Luckily, it's over quickly.

I step over, seeing his skin and bones are melting. I'm not sure how long it will take to completely get rid of him, but I don't care. Yuri isn't here. We found him already and gave him a quick death. I just wanted it over with, so I shot him in the head, execution style.

Amaia never really had a father anyway. She knows I'm here and blames him for everything. She told me she doesn't care how I do it, just to get rid of him. Him dying won't make a difference in our lives, except she will be safer.

We are family now, and one day in the future after she fulfills her dreams, I'll put a baby in her. For now, she has an IUD.

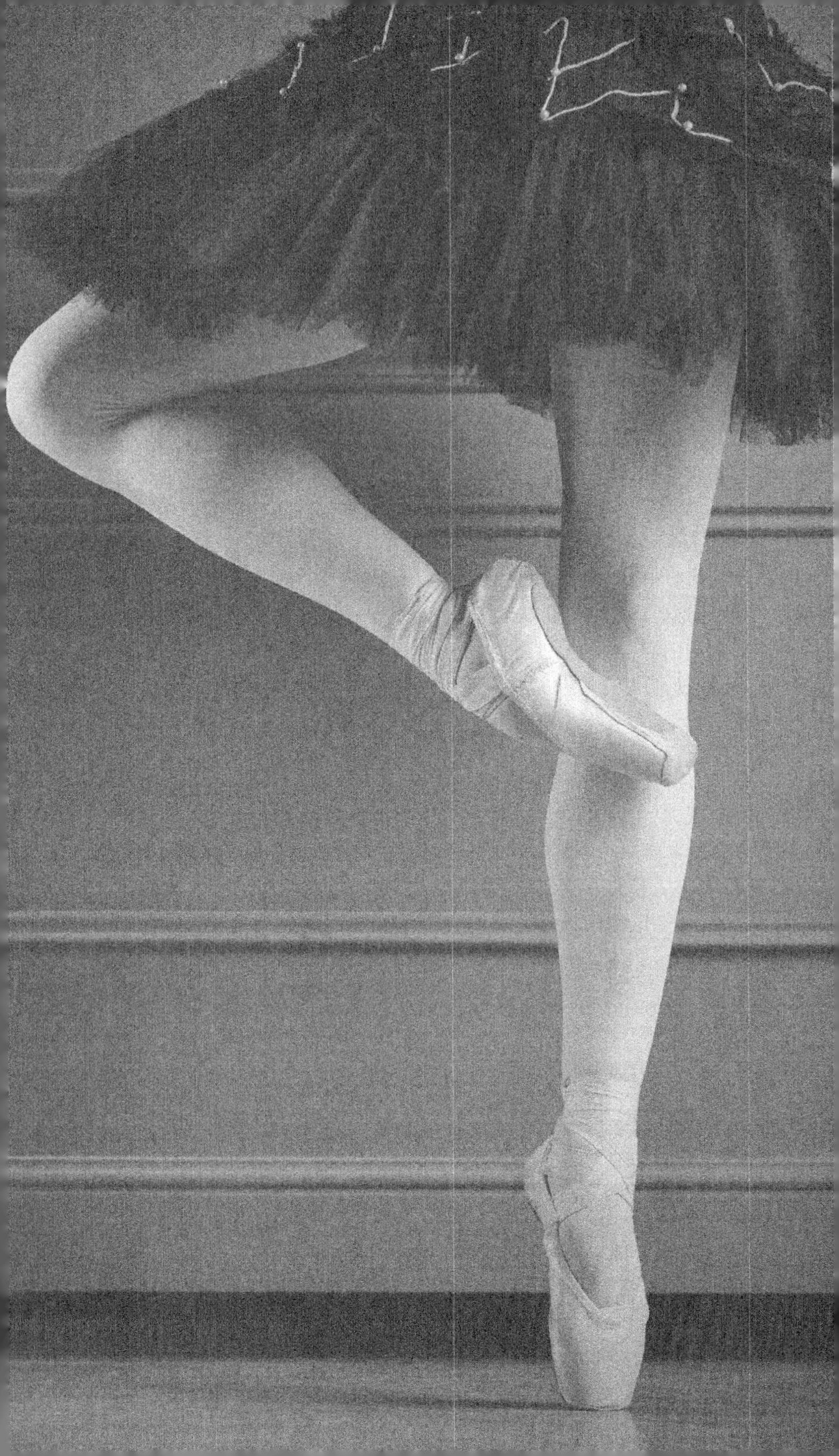

# Chapter Twenty-Six

## Amaia

Konstantin stands next to me in front of the large doors of Viktor's warehouse, and I'm trying to hide my shaking. Nerves are taking over. I twist the ring on my left hand around to help pull me together. To remind me of who I can be, who I am.

This will be the first time I've seen Damien since he attacked me. I wanted to leave seeing him again a couple of weeks until I got my revenge. Thankfully, Viktor was understanding and let me figure things out before I saw him again. He even fed Damien just to keep him alive for me.

We got married in a quick ceremony, and after I meet his family at Christmas, we are going to celebrate it properly. A big wedding, the whole shebang.

My mom will be joining us, too. I also managed to become friends with the girls at the studio. Damien had been feeding them lies to isolate me. But we figured it out after I was chosen for the next Prima. I'm not alone anymore.

The creak of the door pulls me from my thoughts, and Konstantin guides me through without touching me. Damien is tied to a weird-looking chair with straps along his body as well as ankles and wrists.

When he sees me, he begs, "Please don't do this. Don't let him turn you into someone you're not. Ivan said you wanted me and that you weren't allowed to show it in public. I only ever loved you."

He doesn't struggle in the chair; in fact, I don't think he can. I step closer, leaning close to his face, and I laugh. The chair has small nails going through, digging into his skin. There are blood droplets, so I'm guessing at some point he tried to break free.

"You tried to rape me. It's only fair I get some payback, don't you think?" I step toward the toolbox left on the table for me and pull out a hammer.

"He will ruin your future," he pleads while I test the weight of the tool.

"I never forgot my dream. In fact, I've achieved it."

His eyes widen at the realization. "You're the new Prima?"

I nod with a big smile. He opens his mouth to say something else, but I'm done delaying this. I don't want to hear him speak anymore, so I swing the hammer into his kneecap, eliciting an agonized cry. I ignore it and crush the other one. The crack of the bones breaking are drowned out by his screams.

"You crazy bitch," he forces through clenched teeth. I just destroyed his future in dance. One of the things I knew he loved the most.

"The moment you touched me without my permission is the moment you became my enemy."

I'm not done, though. To stop him from touching anyone again, I crush both his hands. The mangled fingers broken and bleeding from being dug into the small nails. This is quite fun.

"Now you can't touch a woman at all," I say, looking back down at the hammer. There is one last place I want to crush. My eyes drop between his legs.

His eyes nearly bulge out of his head. "Please no, not there. I'm sorry, I'm sorry, I'm sorry!"

I ignore his pleas and smash his most precious parts left. I could swear I hear one of his balls popping. He sobs as I chuck the hammer to the side and turn. Walking back to

Konstantin, hiding my pale face.

I thought I'd feel awful after hurting him, but it's mostly relief. I'm my father's daughter after all.

Konstantin stands behind me. "Everything okay?"

I nod. "Yes. Please finish him off however you please. I'll wait in the car."

I walk away and the door closes, my hands rest on my knees and I take a deep breath, needing the small break. When I straighten, I make my way back to the car and slide into the passenger seat. Giving Damien false hope provided me a small amount of satisfaction. Although, I can't imagine a man wanting to live after what I did.

I take deep breaths while I'm waiting and text Viktor.

> I'll be home soon.

> Perfect. See you soon, little doll.

---

Once Viktor is home, he kisses me hard on the lips.

"You okay?" he asks, knowing what I did today.

I bite my lip, "I feel like a weight has been lifted off my shoulders. Thank you for letting me do it on my own."

He tucks a stand of hair behind my ear. "Anything for you. Wife."

I melt into his arms. It felt like a long journey getting here. It's still hard to think about my brother, but Viktor doesn't stop me from mourning. He never told me I couldn't talk about him and our small amount of memories.

He now comes with me to most of my therapist appointments, even if he does sit outside and wait. I've gained a little bit of weight, but it's healthy. It's toning into muscle now. I'm slowly getting used to looking in a full-length mirror without picking things out that are wrong with me.

Viktor comes to all my shows, too. He has never missed a single one. I love him even more for that. Every day feels amazing. He is my support system, and I trust that he would be there for me for anything and everything.

Joan has shown me how to cook some simple and healthy dishes. She was hesitant at first because she's always prepared things herself. But now we enjoy each other's company. She's like an aunt to me. I now have a family I never thought I'd have.

I'm pulling a book from the bookshelf when Viktor come up behind me, holding me close and pressing a small kiss on my neck.

"Christmas is in a couple of weeks. Are you nervous?" Viktor asks when I turn to him, he plays with my necklace. My outdoor collar. He put a tracker inside, and I only ever take it off in our room.

I bite my lip. "A little. I mean, what if they don't like me? We got married without them there. Will they hate me for it?" I've been worrying about it.

He pulls me toward the stairs. "Of course not. They already know." I gasp, and he chuckles, "I couldn't keep it a secret. My father has wanted me to settle down for a while. He is pleased."

I sigh in relief.

"Anyway, if you refuse to come, I will just tie you up and take you there." He throws me over his shoulders and spanks my ass. I wiggle and try to get free, albeit not very hard.

I know where we're going. And I can't wait.

Anticipation runs through me, and I hear the key turn

in the lock of our playroom.

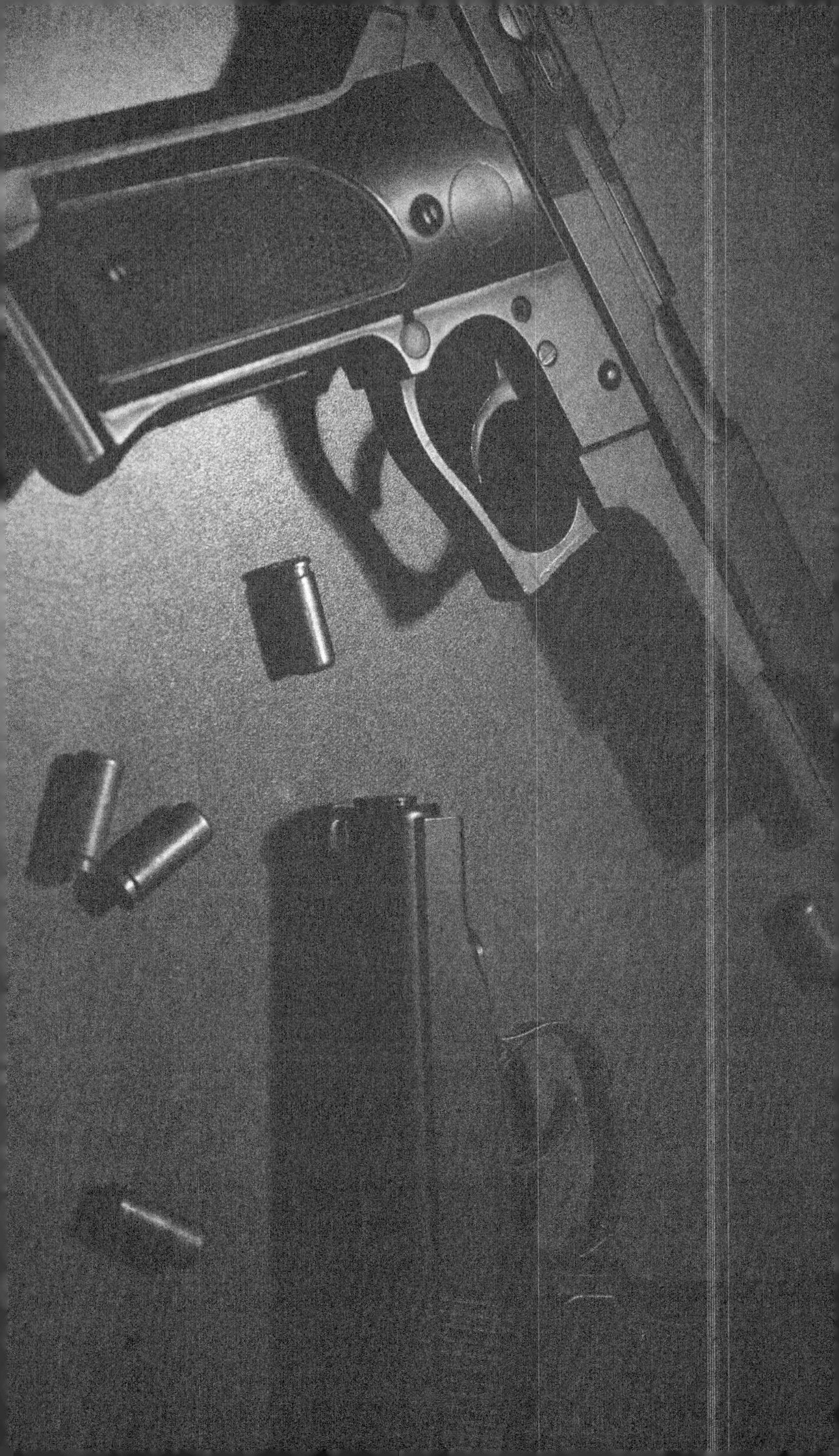

# Epilogue

## Viktor
## Christmas eve

THE SUN HAS SET by the time we arrive outside the large gates of my fathers estate after our flight to Chicago. It's finally time for her to meet my father and brothers this Christmas.

The heavy gates swing open when the security guard types in a code, "Are you ready?" I ask Amaia, as I place my hand on her thigh and circle my thumb. Hoping to calm her nerves.

She had been through a lot recently and I think getting away from California will help her. Be away from the mess. Especially from the memory of Damien.

"Yeah, I think so," she replies, her voice trembling, giving away her nerves.

I pass my fathers mansion and turn to the right, towards

the guest house we will be living in over the holidays. We drive up the long driveway that's decorated by bushes either side of us, the white stucco walls of the mansion come into view. It loomed three stories high.

In my peripheral, I notice Amaia shift and lean forward. "Wow," she whispers.

"You like it? My father had each guest house built for me and my brothers. We will be alone here." I wiggle my eyebrows and her giggle warms my heart.

I park the car in front of the beige garage door, the lights illuminate us, casting a glow over the snow dusting along the ground.

A tall, older man approaches us as I step out and greet him. He has a strong grip. "Good evening Mr Petrov. I hope you had a good journey. I'm here to help you with your bags." I gesture towards the trunk.

I round the car and open the door for Amaia, her eyes are still on the mansion as she clutches onto her purse. "I thought you said it was a guest house?" I wrap my arm around her waist and pull her closer, "It is the guest house." Reaching into the back of the car, I hold onto the large bag full of presents.

The snow crunches under our feet as we step toward the double front doors with a wreath on each one, with lights wrapped around each of the pillars on either side of it.

We enter the foyer, Amaia stares in awe at the decorated Christmas tree tucked in the corner of the curved staircase as I place the bag on the side table. Joyful music plays from another room, jingle bells.

"Better than my house?" I ask teasingly. She blushes and looks away from me. "No, but it's still beautiful."

I pull her up against my body until our faces are inches apart, "This is all material. You are the only beautiful thing in my life. Nothing can ever compare." I brush my nose against hers and kiss her on the lips.

The footsteps on marble pull us away from each other.

"I apologize, Mr Petrov. I'll put these upstairs in the master suite." The tall man ushers past us to the curved stairs with our suitcases in his hand. Amaia stares up at him, "Do you think we should help him?" She asks.

I shake my head and caress her jaw, "no need, he is perfectly happy and paid a substantial amount to be helping us. But give me a minute to send the staff home." I shrug, it's not an inconvenience to me. I'd much rather spend my time alone with my wife.

Amaia moans when I pepper kisses down her throat, "do you want a tour? Or straight to the bedroom," I murmur into her neck. She laughs and moves away. "Tour first?" I feign a whine and she rolls her eyes.

As we travel from room to room, Amaia's eyes roam with wide eyes. I try to see everything from her perspective, excessively decorated with a tree in almost every room. Marble floors and chandeliers. Nothing like her old home and she has never seen my house decorated this much. I kept ours simple since I lived on my own, I never had a reason to decorate like this. For family.

Although I'm mostly looking forward to going to my fathers house where we will be having our meal together. They're all in relationships now too, even my father.

When we walk into the main room, she grabs my hand to get my attention, "Wait, I got you a present and I don't want to wait until tomorrow." Her finger trails down my chest and she plays with the buttons of my shirt.

I raise an eyebrow, not expecting anything, "is it you all wrapped up in a bow?"

She giggles, "No, but maybe I can do that later."

Amaia rushes over to the bag I had left by the door and reaches into it, she pulls out a large golden box, wrapped in a red ribbon and bow. I take it from her hands and hold it carefully, her eyes glisten with excitement. She's almost bouncing on the balls of her feet.

Treating my gift delicately, I pull on the bow until it releases and open the top. A black gun box sits on top of shredded red tissue paper.

"Open it." Amaia urges, holing out her hands and taking the golden box away as I pull out my new gift, I lay it down on the table and flick the gun case open. A silver pistol stares up at me with 'NO MERCY' engraved on the side.

Amaia's small voice pulls me from my staring, "Do you like it?" she asks as she nibbles on her lower lip.

"I love it, it's perfect." I kiss her cheek.

---

A small lady with grey hair walks in, brushing her hands against her white apron, "Good evening Mr Petrov. And Mrs Petrov."

She reminds me of Joan back at my estate.

I shake her hand, "It's nice to meet you, but none of you need to be here from now, take Christmas off. Be with your own families." I give her a kind smile at her and I notice a shine of tears.

"Thank you, sir. Dinner is set on the table." She shuffles away and grabs her coat, giving us one last glance before she rushes out the door.

Amaia wraps her hand around my upper arm, "She will never forget that." Pulling her in close, I press a gentle kiss into her hair. When I see the other members of staff, I will send them all home.

We walk around each room and I dismiss everyone I see, everyone deserves to be with their families for Christmas.

The fireplace has been lit, heating the room. Amaia walks over and holds her hands over it. "This feels nice."

I chuckle, "haven't you been around a natural fire before?"

Amaia shakes her head, "no, we never grew up with a fireplace."

I tilt her chin up so she's looking at me, "It's amazing in the winter, I'm glad to share your first experience." The flickering glow of the flames lights up her face. I couldn't ask for anything more perfect.

She rests her arms around my neck, I lift her up and her legs wrap around my waist, "Merry Christmas," she murmurs, just inches away from my lips.

"I've got a present for you," I tell her with a smirk. After she gave me my perfect gift, I want to give her one. I carry her to the dining room, our meals set up in place with silver domes covering out meals on the top two seats of the table. Candles decorating the middle. But for what I'm about to do, I need to blow them out.

I set Amaia down on the ledge of the table and blow out the candles, the room dims slightly. "We're having dinner?"

She asks and a few strands of hair fall in front of her eyes. I brush them out the way, "not yet, I'm going to eat you first. I've always been a desert man." I tell her as I unbutton her pants. She lifts her hips and I drag them down her thighs.

"Oh yeah?" She asks, licking her lips. I get on my knees and rip the pants past her ankles and chuck them over my shoulder onto the floor. When I look back up at her, her head is tilted backwards and she's panting already. I nip up between her thigh, until I get to her perfect pussy, unfortunately it's covered by lace panties. I'll have to correct that. I tear them off and growl when I notice she's already soaking for me.

Amaia is a goddess.

I don't wait any longer and bury my face between her legs. She tastes absolutely divine. I flick my tongue over her clit and she moans, threading her fingers through my hair and holding me in place. "Don't stop," she pants. I slide my fingers inside her as I suck on her clit and her thighs clench around my head.

I curl my fingers and rub against her g-spot, "that's it, suffocate me, little doll."

Amaia's thighs trembles against me and I know she's close, I pump my fingers faster and with last flick of my tongue, she tightens and comes all over my face. Her fingers grasp harder, giving me a painful sting but I don't care. Her pleasure is mine.

I stay on my knees until she stops shuddering under my touch, my cock is straining against my zipper and it's begging to be inside her. But this isn't about me.

We have come a long way since we first met, a crazy ride and I'll never keep anything from her ever again and never let her out of my sight.

The end.

# Acknowledgements

Thankyou to everyone who has supported me and especially those who are a part of this interconnected family series. Those authors are M.A.Cobb, Luna Mason, Harper-Leigh Rose, M L Hargy and Elle Maldonado.

To my friends who I showed multiple versions of my cover too before deciding on the current one! I must have been annoying with that.

To my Alpha reader, M.A Cobb. I always appreciate every bit of feedback to make my stories better.

To my editor: Ashley, from enchanted author co.

Every one of the girls who is on the group chat who gave me advice and support.

All my ARC readers who gave this novella a chance. I wouldn't have got this far without all of your support and I hope you enjoyed Viktor and Amaia's story.

Last but not least, my partner. Who has dealt with me telling him every detail, giving me time to write and bringing me snacks.

# ALSO BY DARCY

**Wolf shifter**
The wolf's heart

**Italian mafia duet**
Little Sparrow
Sparrow's Revenge

# Petrov Family

**M.A. Cobb**
Nikoli Petrov
**Elle Maldonado**
Mikhail Petrov
Early 2024
**Darcy Embers**
Viktor Petrov
**M.L. Hargy**
Aleksei Petrov
Early 2024
**Harper-Leigh Rose**
Lev Petrov
Early 2024
**Luna Mason**
Roman Petrov
Early 2024

Printed in Great Britain
by Amazon